FINDING THE TREASURE

A COZY QUILTS CLUB MYSTERY

MARSHA DEFILIPPO

To get the latest information on new releases, excerpts and more, be sure to sign up for Marsha's newsletter.

https://marshadefilippo.com/newsletter

PROLOGUE

1926

"Did you hear that?" Nellie Philpot turned from the kitchen sink where she was washing the dinner dishes to face her husband, Franklin "Frank" Philpot.

"All I can hear is wind, rain and thunder," he replied, his head buried in the daily newspaper.

As if to affirm his response, the dark sky lit with a bolt of lightning followed almost immediately with the boom of thunder, rattling the windows and making Nellie jump.

"Oh, my word! That sounds like it must be right over our heads!" she exclaimed. "I thought I heard a knock, but it must have been a tree branch brushing up against the house," she decided aloud and turned back to her dishes. As she did so another bolt of lightning lit the sky and briefly illuminated the view through the kitchen window over the sink and she let out a shriek and clapped her hand over her mouth as the image of a man appeared before her and almost as quickly disappeared.

Frank dropped the newspaper and looked up with concern on his face.

"What's the matter, Nellie?"

"I thought I saw a man outside," she said, her face pale. "I don't see him now, but I swear a face appeared right outside the window. It must have been my imagination, though. I can't see anyone now."

Letting out a grunt of annoyance, Franklin returned to his newspaper as a series of knocks sounded at the front door.

Nellie put her hand to her mouth again and her eyes grew round as she looked questioningly at Frank. He shrugged his shoulders in response to the unasked question of who was at the door.

"Stay here," he told her as he got up and walked to the front of the house where the knocking was emanating. "It must be a stranger in trouble. No one we know ever uses that door."

It might be a uniquely New England rural custom that the front door is rarely ever used and side entrances that most often enter into the kitchen are the preferred route of entry. If someone was at that door it had to be a stranger, and Frank approached cautiously. They lived in a rural area, with the nearest neighbor being half a mile away. He flicked on the switch for the porch light and then pulled aside the curtain covering the sidelight to peer out onto the covered porch. He wanted to take a look at the visitor before opening the door, but if someone was there, he could not see them. He was about to return to the kitchen thinking it must have been their imagination, as the only sounds were the howling wind, pouring rain and rumbling of thunder, not as close now, when there was another knock. He opened the door to find a man, his clothes drenched and clinging to him, leaning against the far side of the door as though he would fall down if he stood upright.

"Please help me. If he catches me, he'll shoot me again. He wants to kill me," he said as his body slid down and fell halfway through the open door.

"Nellie, bring some towels," Frank called out to her as he lifted the man under his arms and pulled him the rest of the way into the house. "And a blanket," he added before turning to close the door and bolt the lock. He gave another quick look out the sidelight, but the darkness and rain made it impossible to see if anyone else was outside. Whoever the man thought was after him was either hiding or not as close as he imagined.

Nellie bustled out of the kitchen. "Who is it, Frank? What's the matter?"

"He's passed out. He said someone's after him and trying to kill him. You go after the towels and blanket and I'll move him onto the couch in the living room."

She gave the man a quick look before passing by them and up the stairs to the linen closet. By the time she returned with them, Frank had dragged the still unconscious man into the living room and had removed his shoes, but he was still on the floor.

"Lay some towels down first. This guy is soaked to the bones. Why don't you put on the teakettle and I'll try to dry him off some before I do that. Maybe he'll wake up and be able to get himself up on the couch. A hot cup of tea might help him warm up."

Curious, but not wanting to be in the room while he dried the man off just in case he had to remove any of his clothing, Nellie returned to the kitchen and filled the teakettle and set it on the stove. She heard a soft moaning and then a cry of pain, and hurried back into the living room to find out what was happening. Frank had taken off the man's shirt and trousers, but he was still in his underclothes. The man had his arm around Frank's shoulder and Frank was supporting him around the waist as he lowered him onto the couch, where he had spread some towels. Once the man was safely settled, he covered him with the blanket. They had been facing away from her when she'd entered the room, but as Frank was lowering him onto the couch, she saw the blotch of red on the man's undershirt that was obviously fresh blood.

"Oh, Frank! He's hurt."

"He's been shot," he replied, his mouth set. "You'll need to bring some bandages. Lots of them. As many as you can find."

Nellie ran from the room and up the stairs to their first aid supplies. Having a generous supply of bandages on hand was a necessity at a working farm, and Nellie was glad she'd recently replenished their stock. Grabbing the basket with the gauze and tape, she hurried back down the stairs. Frank was lifting the undershirt as gently as possible, but the man let out a cry of pain when it pulled away from his skin where the bullet had entered. As Nellie laid the basket on the floor next to Frank, the whistling of the teakettle alerted her it was ready.

"Don't put anything on the wound until I come back with the water. You'll need to wash away the blood first. It looks like it's not bleeding bad now, but you don't want it to get infected. I'll bring the iodine, too." She hurried back to the kitchen to take the angrily whistling kettle off the stove and was about to pour some into a bowl before changing her mind. Better to take the kettle with her and use one of the biggest mixing bowls. She grabbed clean dishcloths from the drawer and the bottle of iodine she kept on the window ledge above the sink and put them into the bowl so she could carry the kettle in her other hand. That wound was going to need a thorough washing. It seemed like she'd taken forever, but was only minutes until she reappeared in the living room to help Frank. He had retrieved the bottle of whiskey they kept for entertaining from the dining room and poured two fingers' worth into a glass which the man was drinking, grimacing either from pain or the whiskey. Nellie wasn't sure which.

"Thanks," he said between clenched teeth as he handed the empty glass back to Frank and then collapsed back onto the couch.

"I'm sorry. This is probably going to hurt but we need to get that wound cleaned and bandaged," Nellie told him as she put the supplies on the floor and lowered to her knees on the floor beside him. "Who did this to you?"

"Thanks. Just do what you need to do. I can take it," the man replied, but avoided answering her question.

She decided to let that go. "What's your name?" she asked instead, looking up at Frank in case he had already asked, but he shook his head.

"Frank. Frank Abbott."

"Well, what a coincidence. My husband's name is Frank, too," Nellie replied cheerily as she gently dabbed at the now dried blood farthest away from the hole in the man's side.

His body jerked as she got closer to the wound, but then stiffened and he clenched his teeth to hold back from crying out. She debated whether to keep talking and decided it might be best to try to take the man's mind off her ministrations.

"This has to be the worst storm we've had in years. I can't remember it raining this hard or the wind howling so much. Can you, Franklin?" She looked up at him and smiled.

He looked at her as though she'd gone mad and then realized what she was doing.

"No, can't say as I have. Can't imagine why anyone would be out on a night like this," he added. "What had you out, Frank?"

Frank's eyes had been tightly shut and the muscles in his jaw twitched from being clenched, but he opened them to look up at Franklin as though deciding whether to tell the truth. Franklin returned his gaze and remained quiet, but his demeanor told Frank that it wouldn't be wise to lie. He swallowed and took a deep breath to settle himself both for the pain and for what he was about to say.

"There are... were... three of us. We had a treasure map and were following the clues. Harvey had won it in a poker game. The guy who lost told him it had belonged to a pirate named Dixie Bull who was in Maine in the 1600s. We had two boats and were traveling up the Penobscot River and then to the Kenduskeag. John was in his copper bottom boat and Harvey and I were in the other one. We figured we'd need one just for the gold once we'd found it. Gold can be real heavy. A lot heavier than you'd think," he said by way of explanation for why they'd need an extra boat. "We each had a piece of the map so no one would pull a double-cross, but Harvey did anyway." His eyes turned hard. "Once we got to the spot where it looked like the gold would be buried and had pulled the boats up onto shore, he shot John and killed him. He would have killed me, too, but I was able to get a punch in and knocked him down and started running. That's when he shot me. The first one just grazed my arm, but he shot again and got me in my side. I didn't know where I was going, but just kept running until I thought I lost him. I didn't hear him coming after me, but then it got dark, and the storm came in. I'm lucky I found your house," he finished, his voice growing weaker as he spoke, and his eyes fluttered.

"You just rest now, Frank. The bleeding seems to have stopped, but you should probably stay still. Would you like a cup of tea? Something warm might help you feel better."

"No, thanks, ma'am. I think I'd just like to sleep awhile if that's okay with you."

"Of course. I'll get another blanket for you. You're starting to shiver," Nellie told him and looked at Franklin, who nodded in agreement, as she left the room. Once she returned and had tucked the quilt around Abbott, who had already fallen asleep, she and Franklin went into the kitchen out of earshot.

"The phone line must be down from the storm. I tried to call the sheriff while you were getting the quilt but couldn't raise the operator. I should go for the sheriff, but I don't want to leave you alone in case his partner... Harvey?" he asked, and Nellie nodded, "is still looking for him."

"Oh, yes, please don't leave me alone," Nellie said, her face showing her fear.

Franklin took her in his arms and held her close to reassure her.

"We'll just have to wait until morning and figure it out then. Maybe he will have his strength back after a good night's sleep and leave on his own. You go on to bed now. The doors are all locked and I have my hunting rifle and will stand guard."

She looked into his eyes, debating internally whether to argue, but she knew how stubborn he could be once he'd made up his mind to do something.

"Alright, I'll go to bed, but I'm not sure that I'll be able to sleep."

He smiled before telling her, "That's okay. You give it a try, anyway." He kissed the top of her head before releasing her from their embrace. "Go on now."

The night passed without incident and despite his best efforts, Franklin had dozed off in the chair he'd placed facing Frank Abbott, and with a line of sight toward the front door. As soon as he woke, he was aware something was wrong. He got up and walked over to the couch where Frank was still lying on his back and when he looked at his face, it was obvious he was dead but checked his pulse just to make sure. He pulled the quilt up over Frank's face so that Nellie wouldn't have to see; then went to the kitchen to check the phone and the operator came on the line.

"Sally, this is Franklin Philpot. Would you tell the sheriff we need him to come to our house?"

"Sure, Franklin. Is something wrong?"

Knowing they were on a party line, and it was possible others were listening in, he avoided a direct answer. "Tell him it's no hurry, but we'll need to see him as soon as he's able to drop by," and then hung up.

He went into the dining room and gathered up Abbott's clothing, which Nellie had placed over the backs of the chairs to dry. In the pocket of Abbott's trousers, he found a wallet and inside was a folded piece of paper. He unfolded it and discovered it was what appeared to be a piece of a hand-drawn map. Abbott must have been telling the truth after all. Franklin tucked the paper into his own trousers as Nellie came down the stairs.

"Abbott is dead," he told her. "I've had Sally call the sheriff. We'll tell him what Abbott told us. I'm not sure it's going to help much since he didn't give us any full names other than his own and we don't know what direction he was coming from."

"But I thought he was just tired and needed rest last night," Nellie objected.

"He must have lost too much blood or gone into shock. He never woke up that I'm aware of."

Franklin took her arm and gently led her into the kitchen away from the body, where they both waited for the sheriff to arrive.

He never mentioned to her that he had taken the map and put it in the hidden compartment of the case that held his watch, tie clips, and cufflinks. But the story about the night Frank Abbott had shown up on their doorstep during one of the worst storms in decades, shot, and talking about buried gold and a copper bottom boat, was retold many times over the years and passed down through the generations.

CHAPTER ONE

~

"*D*oes anyone have an idea for a new project?" Annalise Jordan asked the other three women assembled for the meeting of the Cozy Quilts Club, which was held at the house of Eva Perkins. It had been Eva's idea to form the club after they'd all taken a quilting class together at the Quilting Essentials quilt shop, and the group decided they would like to continue meeting even after the class was over.

"I've been looking online at the tutorials made by Sandy Fischer at Classic Quilts to see if I could come up with some ideas," Jennifer Ryder said.

"I *love* her tutorials!" Sarah Pascal said. "She can make the hardest blocks so simple to sew with the way she breaks them down. And her videos are always entertaining and easy to understand."

"I agree. I've been watching them for years," Eva said.

"I didn't come up with anything specific to suggest, but if anyone else has ideas, I'm open to them," Jennifer put in.

"That's a great idea. What do you think, Reuben?" Eva looked at her Maine coon cat sitting by her chair, who looked back at her with what could only be described as disgust before getting to his feet and returning to his cushion in the bay window.

"I guess he doesn't feel like sharing today," Annalise said, and the others chuckled.

What the members of the Cozy Quilts Club hadn't realized before forming the club and their first meeting the month before was that each of them had a paranormal ability. Annalise had been the first to realize and mention it. Her abilities were of the psychic variety and Eva's was communicating with animals. Sarah communicated with ghosts a la The Sixth Sense and Jennifer's skill was psychometry. They'd used their abilities to solve the murder of Jennifer's great-aunt, Sadie, the previous month.

"He's been in a snooty mood today, even for a cat," Eva replied. Reuben turned his head and glared at Eva. "See what I mean?" she said and chuckled again.

They tossed around ideas for the next half hour but couldn't decide on one that hit the spot for all of them.

"Why don't we adjourn for tonight and we can each watch some videos or go through our quilt books to revisit this next week? Eva suggested.

"Sounds like a plan," Annalise replied. Jennifer and Sarah nodded in agreement.

"Meeting adjourned. We've still got some time before we usually finish up. How about we go out on the patio and enjoy the evening for a bit? I don't think the mosquitoes and black flies are too bad, and I made a batch of peanut butter cookies earlier today. I need some help eating them."

"You don't have to ask me twice," Jennifer said, licking her lips.

"Or me," both Sarah and Annalise said at the same time, and followed Eva and Jennifer to the patio.

CHAPTER TWO

~

The next morning, Annalise was settled in her bedroom sitting room that faced the back of her property. It was her favorite spot in her house and provided a view out across the expanse of lawn and gardens that stretched out several hundred feet, ending where they met a line of trees. On the other side of the trees was the Kenduskeag River, but even from her second-story window it was not visible. When she wanted to be by the water, she used the path worn into the landscape by the footsteps of previous generations of her family who had lived on the property. She'd spent countless hours exploring the woods and shoreline over the years as this was the house she had grown up in and recently inherited after the passing of her parents. Her mother had been the last to die the previous year. Annalise already owned a home, but it was the one she had lived in with her husband, Peter. Peter had been the love of her life but had been killed in an automobile accident when she was 30 and she had never remarried. Once her grief had mellowed, she had tried dating, but no one ever appealed to her the way Peter had and eventually she stopped even trying. She was comfortable with her life as a single woman. Even though the farmhouse had more square footage than one person needed, it felt right to move back in rather than sell it. If she had any regret about her circumstances, it would be that she had never had any children to pass the homestead onto.

The house was a New England farmhouse style built in the 1800s, with a large wraparound porch on two sides of the building. On the first floor was a kitchen, dining room, living room, and what would have been called a parlor at the time it was built. The proceeds from the sale of her house had enabled her to resign from the job she'd held for the last thirty years as a secretary at the University of Maine and work part-time, pursuing her passion as a Reiki practitioner. She had used a portion of the proceeds to convert the parlor into her office, where clients came for Reiki sessions and added a half bathroom so they would not have to go upstairs if they needed to use the facilities. The original floor plan of the second floor included four bedrooms, but she converted one into a large primary en suite and sitting room.

She was reading the morning edition of The Bangor News with her second cup of coffee when she spotted a story that caught her attention. Looking at the byline, she recognized the name of the reporter, Susan Reynolds. She had met Susan the year before when Susan was doing a story about alternative medicine and holistic practices. A mutual friend had suggested Susan contact her to discuss Reiki and what was involved with a session. At first, Annalise wasn't sure if it would be beneficial, as many journalists disregarded any practices not based totally on science and traditional Western modern medicine. After meeting Susan, though, she felt confident she was keeping an open mind, so agreed to the interview. She was in her mid-40s and still single, pretty, with natural blonde hair and blue eyes and by no means a fluff reporter. Annalise found Susan to be all business and single-minded about her career, but had a fun side which she showed once the interview was over. As part of the interview, Annalise had suggested that she give Susan a reiki session so that she could experience it firsthand. Susan had told her once the session was over that she had expected to feel nothing, but wouldn't have felt she'd done her job if she hadn't tried it herself. To her surprise, the relaxing atmosphere of the room and Annalise's expert guidance had brought out emotions she had thought long buried. When Annalise shared the impressions she had received while performing the session, including a revelation no one else would have known about, Susan was a believer. She had been a regular client ever since, as well as a good friend.

THE HEADLINE READ:

SKELETAL REMAINS FOUND under copper-bottomed boat in Kenduskeag River

THE SUMMER HAD BEEN ESPECIALLY hot and dry, and drought conditions were common in several of the counties. The water level of many of the lakes and streams around the state had dipped to record lows, and many items that had once been submerged were now resurfacing.

Annalise felt the tingle that told her this was a story she should continue to read.

IN A MACABRE TWIST, the skeletal human remains of a man who appears to have been shot were found underneath what authorities are speculating is a copper bottom boat in the Kenduskeag River. The boat had been submerged in a remote area that was not suitable for building and had been hidden until the recent drought made it visible. It was discovered by two teenagers exploring the shoreline who made the grisly discovery when they decided to turn the boat over to see if it would still float. The State Crime Lab has recovered the remains and will try to determine if there is DNA that would make it possible to learn the identity of the man. It appears the boat may have been there since the 1920s, which may make identification impossible, but the popularity of DNA testing has widened the scope of information available for authorities to match relatives to cold case victims. We will keep you updated if more information becomes available.

THE WORDS "COPPER BOTTOM BOAT" niggled at Annalise's memory. It sounded familiar, but she couldn't quite place it. She returned to reading the other articles in the paper when suddenly it came to her. It was the story her father, Ralph Philpot, had told which he had heard from his father, Elmo. On a stormy night in 1926, a stranger had shown up on her great-grandparents' door in this very house. The stranger claimed to have been shot by his partner, who had also killed another man when they were looking for buried gold. The stranger had died in the night and the police never found the person who had shot him. She remembered being told something about a copper bottom boat, and when she was a little girl, Annalise's father had shown her the piece of the map which had been found in the stranger's pocket. He had discovered it in a hidden compartment of a jewelry box passed onto him by his father. Remembering this, she went to look for the box with her father's belongings which her mother had stored in the attic.

"I really do need to go through these boxes," she thought to herself when she opened the door to the attic. It was still early enough in the day that the temperature in the space hadn't approached the stifling heat of late afternoon in mid-summer. The slightly musty smell of decades of articles stored in the boxes wasn't unpleasant. To Annalise, it had a sense of comfort and brought back memories of lives well-lived and shared connections with her ancestors which wrapped around her like a warm blanket. The attic floor was scattered with an assortment of boxes, Christmas ornaments and other holiday decorations which should probably be discarded, but her mother had wanted to keep for sentimental reasons, along with clothing she would never have a use for. Fortunately, her mother had at least labeled the boxes, so she was able to find the right one after having to only move a few of them out of the way. The box contained a packet of letters her parents had exchanged when her father was serving in the Army during the Korean War, along with some of his clothing. She held one of his shirts to her nose but was disappointed to find it no longer had her father's scent. She removed those and set them aside and then at the bottom of the carton, she saw the wooden box that had been passed from father to son since her grandfather's time. Opening the lid, she found the cuff links and tie clips which had also been passed down. The compartment had a spring mechanism which opened by pushing down the top tray, and she tried doing that. It seemed to be stuck at first, but she tried one more time and the tray rose slightly, indicating the spring had released and she lifted it out. A piece of folded, yellowed paper was in the hidden compartment. She pulled it out with one hand and then set the jewelry box on the floor so she could open the paper. It was the map. Annalise drew in her breath, not quite believing after all these years, the story she'd been told might be true. How many copper-bottomed boats could there be, though, and the skeletal remains had to be those of the partner who'd been shot and killed. She put the clothing and letters back in the box and returned the map to the hidden compartment before inserting the tray and pushing it down so the spring would engage and lock it once again. It might be nothing or not even related at all to the story in the paper, but she decided to call Susan Reynolds and share it anyway. What she did with it would be up to her.

CHAPTER THREE

~

*S*he pressed Call from her Contacts list, half expecting to be directed to Susan's voice mail, so was surprised when Susan answered on the second ring.

"Annalise, it's good to hear from you. Do you need to reschedule our next session?"

"No, we're still good for our appointment. I'm calling about the piece you did for The Bangor News about the skeletal remains found under a boat."

"Really?" Susan asked with a mixture of surprise and curiosity.

"I thought you might be interested to learn more about this," and proceeded to relate to Susan the story she had been told about a stormy night in 1926 when a man showed up on her great-grandparents' doorstep with a wild story about being shot by his partner while they were looking for buried gold.

"And you have a piece of the treasure map?" Susan asked when Annalise had finished.

"Yes, it was in a box with my father's belongings stored in

the attic. It was still in my father's jewelry box and if I'm remembering correctly, it had originally belonged to my great-grandfather. It has a hidden compartment where the map has been all this time." Annalise was about to tell Susan how the tray for the jewelry operated to reveal the hidden compartment below, but stopped when she felt the strong intuitive signal that always meant she should listen. What she sensed was that this piece of information should remain private.

"This is amazing," Susan said. "Do you mind if I do a follow-up story with what you've told me?"

"Of course, if you think it might help identify the person they found. To the best of my recollection, we only had the name of the person who showed up at my great-grandparents' house, which I've already given you, and the first names of his fellow treasure hunters, so it might not end up being helpful especially after all this time. But there's always a chance someone else knows about this and will make a connection just as I did. My spidey senses are telling me the information about the jewelry box having a secret compartment shouldn't be released to the public, though, so that's off the record."

"Of course. I completely understand your hesitation. The follow-up story should be in the paper in the next couple of days."

"I'll be looking for it!"

CHAPTER FOUR

～

"I've got some exciting news to share with you!" Annalise announced at the next meeting of the Cozy Quilts Club. "And I think I've found a quilt design for our next project. That is, unless someone else has come up with a better idea they'd like to do…" she looked around at the others gathered around the table.

Eva was the first to reply. "I didn't come up with anything that couldn't be done later, and you seem pretty excited about this."

"Yes, tell us your idea," Sarah seconded, and Jennifer nodded her agreement.

"Well, this is going to require a bit of backstory," Annalise began and then told them the tale about the events in 1926 and her discovery of the map piece still hidden in her father's jewelry box.

"Wow! That's quite a story," Sarah said when Annalise had finished.

"It doesn't end there. Did any of you hear about the skeletal remains found under a copper bottom boat in the Kenduskeag River? The Bangor News did a story about it a couple days ago and I happen to know Susan Reynolds, who was the reporter. I contacted her and told her this story and that I have part of the map, although I asked her to leave out the part about the secret compartment in the jewelry box. My intuition told me I shouldn't share that bit of information publicly. Anyway, she's running the follow-up story this week, possibly even tomorrow."

"I'll be sure to read it," Eva said. "And not just because it's you, although that makes it even more interesting. I love mysteries."

"Which brings me back to the connection to my quilt project idea," Annalise continued. "After talking to Susan, I did an internet search for quilt blocks with the word treasure in them and the results popped up with a tutorial for a quilt called Treasure Box. After our discussion last week about Sandy Fischer's tutorials, I thought it was serendipity. She's done it as a small quilt which could be used as a wall hanging or lap quilt, I guess, but it looks like it would be easy to make it bigger. I also can picture it being made narrower and longer to use as a table runner. I printed a picture of the quilt to show you and wrote down the URL for the tutorial if you want to check it out online."

"I'll get my laptop and we can do that right now," Eva offered.

"Thanks, Eva. I'd love to watch the tutorial before making a final decision, but on the surface, it sounds like it would be fun, especially with Annalise's treasure connection. Did they ever actually find the gold?" Jennifer asked.

"My grandparents didn't know. The man who showed up died before they were able to ask him any more about what happened that night, and he didn't have anything with him. Chances are it was all bogus, anyway. I mean, what are the chances of there being a stash of buried gold in this part of the state?"

"Did your grandparents or father ever try to find it?" Sarah asked.

"My father went out to where he thought the guy might have come from. He took a metal detector with him, but he didn't find anything and without the other pieces of the map, he wasn't sure he was actually in the right area. He gave it up after spending one entire summer going out whenever he had some free time. I think my mother might have had something to say about all the time he was putting into it and leaving us alone," Annalise said, a smile on her face at the memory of her mother chastising her father.

Eva returned with her laptop and brought up the tutorial. After watching it, they all agreed the Treasure Box pattern would be perfect for their next project.

CHAPTER FIVE

~

$\mathcal{A}$nnalise was in her usual spot the next morning when her phone rang, and Eva's number showed up on the screen.

"Good morning! You're up early," Annalise greeted her.

"If you're not busy today, I thought we could take a trip to Quilting Essentials to pick out fabric for the Treasure Box project. Unless you already have fabric on hand."

"Oh, I do, but you don't have to twist my arm to take a trip to check out new fabric. The store won't be open until 9:30. Have you had breakfast? We could meet at The Checkout Diner first."

"That's a great idea. I haven't had breakfast yet and having someone else make it for me isn't something I turn down often."

Annalise laughed. "Great! I'll meet you at the diner. Can you be there in fifteen minutes?"

"I can and will, with bells on!"

"Perfect. See you there."

Annalise pulled into the parking lot just as Eva was getting out of her car. The diner had an attached convenience store, which made it a favorite destination for the community. It was small, but the food was always delicious and reasonably priced. Sometimes that meant it could be packed, but it looked like they had hit it at a good time. Only one other booth was occupied when they stepped inside.

"I'll be right with you. Just grab a spot wherever you want to sit," Betty Jones called to them as she headed toward the kitchen with a stack of dishes she'd cleaned from the table whose occupants were just leaving.

"I read the piece in The Bangor News about your family's adventure with the treasure hunter back in the day. That was quite a story," Betty greeted Annalise when she returned with menus and filled their mugs with coffee.

"I didn't realize it was in the paper today. As I told Susan Reynolds, I have no idea if any of it is true, but it seemed more than coincidental when I read the article about the skeleton and copper bottom boat."

"If it wasn't for the recent drought lowering the water level and exposing the boat, you might never have known for sure," Eva said.

"And the story would have died with me, as I'd never shared it with anyone before."

"So your great-grandparents never mentioned if the killer came around to find out what they knew?" Betty asked.

"No, but what happened wasn't reported to the public that I'm aware of. The Sheriff's office sent someone out to take Frank Abbott's body away, but he wasn't a local, so it wasn't as easy in those days to track people down and it never got reported to a newspaper. The killer had to have somehow dumped the other body and the boat in the river, since no one was able to find it when they looked in likely locations Frank Abbott might have been. He hadn't provided enough detail for them to know for sure which direction he'd come from. My understanding is they didn't put a lot of time into looking, and they concluded the killer must have left town to avoid being captured. Chances are the killer didn't spend much time looking for Frank once he'd gotten rid of the other body and boat. From what my great-grandparents had said, there was a terrible storm that night so it must have made it too difficult to track him and as I said, he probably also wanted to get out of town as quickly as possible just in case the police had been notified."

"After all this time, they probably don't have any evidence with DNA, so finding any relatives now is unlikely even though they have the technology," Eva said.

"Sounds like it's a mystery that may never be solved. In the meantime, what can I get you two besides coffee?" Betty asked.

They gave her their orders and Betty bustled off to the kitchen.

Annalise and Eva finished their breakfast amid discussions of quilting and, saying their goodbyes to Betty, they headed to Quilting Essentials.

"Hello, ladies," Evelyn Jackson, the owner, greeted them with a smile. "We got a new shipment of fabrics in yesterday. They're on the display stand near the batiks and we're running a twenty percent off sale on the cotton solids on the back wall. Are you here just to browse, or do you have a special project in mind?"

"The Cozy Quilters are going to do variations of the Treasure Box design from one of Classic Quilt's tutorials. Are you familiar with it?" Annalise asked.

"I can't say I am, but I do love Sandy Fischer's tutorials," Evelyn replied.

"I brought a printout of the PDF with the dimensions and fabric needed," Annalise said as she opened her purse and pulled it out to show Evelyn.

"Oh, I see. Yes, it would be very easy to adapt this design's length or width," Evelyn said after studying the illustration of the quilt.

"I was thinking I would make a table runner instead, so I would only put three blocks across, but use the remaining blocks from this to add to the length. I'm going to need your help to make sure I have enough fabric for the borders since it won't match what's on the PDF," Eva said.

"And I want to do a throw, which will mean more blocks than this, but the design lends itself to easily adding more both to the width and length, so it shouldn't be a problem, other than doing the math."

"That's no problem at all. I've got an app for that!" Evelyn said.

"Somehow, I knew you would!" Annalise replied, and everyone laughed.

They spent the next hour looking through the fabric selections, batting, and thread and with purchases in hand, left the store eager to begin their projects.

"This was a great idea, Eva. I don't know why I ever buy fabric unless I'm going to do a specific project. It seems like I always buy more instead of using what I already have on hand."

"You're not alone. I promise myself repeatedly I will shop from my stash, but it rarely happens. I love this new fabric, though. It's going to be perfect for my dining room."

"You have a good rest of the day. I'm heading home to start mine," Annalise said, tossing her bag in the back seat of her car and waving goodbye.

"Me, too!"

CHAPTER SIX

⌇

*T*wo days later, Annalise was in the checkout lane at the grocery store when she felt the familiar prickle which signaled she was about to receive information, and a vision of her living room in a state of complete disarray came to her. Books had been pulled from their shelves and were strewn on the floor. The cushions on her couch were also on the floor. The scene changed to her bedroom, and she saw the drawers pulled open and the contents dumped on the floor. Her closet was a shambles with what had been on the shelves above her clothing pulled down, boxes opened and discarded on the floor.

"Are you alright?" the cashier asked, worry showing on her face.

Annalise brought her attention back to her surroundings.

"I'm... I'm fine, but I need to go home. I think someone has broken into my house."

The cashier gave her an odd look but bagged her groceries and completed the transaction. With a quick thank you, Annalise hurried to her car, depositing the groceries in the trunk. She scanned her body to get a sense of whether the intruder—assuming there was one, or this had even been a vision of the current moment—might still be in her house. Despite feeling uneasy, she knew deep down that no one was in her house, but she called Eva anyway.

"I'm on my way home from the grocery store and should be there within fifteen minutes. I don't want to call the police just in case I'm wrong and my vision wasn't true, but I think someone has broken into my house. Are you able to meet me there?"

"Oh, my goodness! Of course! Jim is here with me now. I'll bring him with me. We should arrive about the time you do...." Eva's voice became muffled, and Annalise could tell she was speaking to Jim now when she heard her say, "It's Annalise. She thinks someone may have broken into her house and asked if I would come to be with her."

"Tell her not to go inside until we get there," Annalise heard Jim saying in the background.

"Did you hear Jim?"

"I did. I'll wait in my car and if I see a strange car in the driveway, I'll drive a little farther up the road and park on the shoulder."

Jim Davis, Eva's partner, was a retired state police officer and knowing that settled Annalise's nerves, reassuring her she would be safe. Feeling better knowing she wouldn't be going into the situation by herself, Annalise parked in her driveway. No car was parked anywhere near her house, but she stayed in her car and looked around in case someone was hiding. She hadn't seen anyone either behind or on the side of the house away from the driveway as she'd approached the house, but better to wait for Eva and Jim.

They arrived within minutes of Annalise's arrival. They all gathered behind her car to discuss the best approach.

"Thank you so much for coming. I haven't gone in yet."

"I'm glad you waited. It doesn't look like anyone is here, but better to be safe than sorry," Jim told her. "Why don't you give me your house key and I'll go in first while you two wait on the porch or in the car? I'll come back out after I've searched the rooms, and it's safe to come in."

Annalise nodded in agreement, too shaken to say more.

Five very long minutes later, Jim came outside and waved an all clear before joining them at the cars.

"You were right. Someone has been here and made quite a mess. I've called 911 and an officer is on the way. How long had you been gone?"

"Not long. I only went into the grocery store to pick up a few items. I'd guess maybe forty-five minutes to an hour at the most with the travel time to and from the store."

"They must have been watching the house and waiting until you left to go through it the way they did and be gone by the time we got here."

"How bad is it?" Eva asked.

"They don't seem to have broken anything, so not that kind of damage, but they must have been looking for something specific based on how they've left things and what they chose to go through. It might have been someone looking for valuables to sell for drug money."

They spotted the police car approaching and slowing down to pull into the driveway. Jim waved to the officer getting out when he recognized who it was.

"Jim, I didn't expect to find you here," Deputy Tremblay said as he walked toward them.

"I'm here for moral support. You've met Eva, and this is Annalise Jordan, the homeowner. Annalise, this is Deputy Carl Tremblay."

"Nice to meet you," she said as they shook hands. "Thank you for coming out so quickly."

"Dispatch said this is a break-in," he said, more as a question.

"That's right. I haven't been inside yet, but Jim has. He told me it looks as though whoever broke in was looking for something specific, but I'll have to go inside to check whether anything has been taken. My intuition is telling me they were looking for the jewelry box. I realize even if they have taken it, chances of recovering it are slim. No offense intended toward the Sheriff's office."

"None taken. Unfortunately, that's true more often than not. What jewelry box?"

"It was mentioned in the article Susan Reynolds did about my family having a piece of a treasure map which might have been connected to the skeleton those two boys found under a boat in the river. It's not important for you to have all the details if you didn't read it, though."

"Fair enough. Why don't we go inside and take a look? Do you know how they got in?"

"No, I stayed outside and haven't looked at the side or back entrance or windows. Should we start with that?"

"It looks like they may have jimmied a window in the back. I'm guessing you wouldn't have left it open without the screen on this time of year," he said, addressing Annalise.

"No, I wouldn't have, and I confess in the warmer months, I'm not as careful about remembering to lock them after I've closed them back up at the end of the day. I thought they were all closed before I went to bed last night, though. At least the ones downstairs."

Deputy Tremblay led the way into the house, with Annalise close behind.

CHAPTER SEVEN

⁓

*A*nnalise gasped and put her hand to her mouth when she walked into her living room. Just as it had been in her vision, the bookcases had all been emptied onto the floor, along with the cushions on the couch and chairs. Nothing appeared to be missing, though.

"I don't think anything is missing in this room."

"It didn't look like they'd been in your Reiki studio, but they've been upstairs in your bedroom."

This time Annalise led the way, and everyone followed.

As before, her bedroom looked like it had in her vision, but the shock didn't affect her as viscerally as it had when she saw the disarray in her living room. She walked around the room, picking up clothing here and there, checking for anything hidden underneath, but it appeared to all be clothing. Next, she went to her bureau, where she kept her jewelry box. It had been turned upside down and the contents dumped on the top of her bureau. Most of Annalise's jewelry had no significant monetary or senti-mental value, so it did not surprise her nothing had been taken.

She stepped into her walk-in closet where the clothes had been pushed to one side as though the burglars were looking for perhaps a safe or hidden compartment, although there were neither. Her extra handbags had been tossed on the floor, but they all appeared to be accounted for. She walked into her sitting room and her eyes immediately went to the side table where she had placed the jewelry box containing her father's (and his father's and his father's father before him) cuff links and tie clips. They had been removed and were lying on the table next to the now empty box. Her intuition told her it was the map they were looking for. She rushed to the box and pressed down on the top tray to release the catch of the hidden compartment. Still where she'd left it was the treasure map. The thieves obviously didn't know about the secret compartment, and she was grateful now she listened to her intuition and hadn't told that part of the story to Susan Reynolds.

"This is what they were looking for," she said, turning to face the others with the paper in her hand. "They must have read the story in the paper or heard about it somehow and came here to steal the treasure map."

"That has to be why nothing is missing," Eva said. "They must have worked their way up to this room in case you had hidden it in the other rooms instead of coming directly to your bedroom... which would have been the logical place to look," she added, more as an aside.

"But if it is what they were looking for, will they try coming back, is the question," Jim said. "You might want to think about installing some security measures, just in case."

Annalise's face paled and Eva came over to comfort her.

"Maybe you should come home with us and stay the night," she offered.

Annalise considered the offer, but decided she wasn't going to let someone scare her out of her own house. She'd just have to do better about locking all her windows and doors. Having a home security system installed might not be a bad idea, though.

"I appreciate the offer, but I'll be alright."

"Are you sure?" Eva asked with a frown on her face.

"I'm sure. It's going to take me a while to pick everything up and put it back in its place, and I'd rather not come home to this mess again tomorrow."

"Tell you what. Jim and I will help you, and then you can stay overnight with me. We don't know if the thieves gave up or were interrupted somehow. They might come back again and if you're home..." Eva let that scenario play out in Annalise's head.

"You're right," she sighed. "I don't want to let them frighten me out of my own house, but it could be dangerous if I am here alone in the middle of the night, and they come back. Especially since I don't really know if it's just one person. Not that I would be able to fight off even one person, but my chances go down significantly if it is more than one."

"Then it's a plan. Let's clean this place up."

"Sounds like there's nothing else I can do, so I should be on my way," Deputy Tremblay said.

"Thank you again for coming and if there's any way you could leave out the treasure map in your report..."

"What treasure map?" he asked, giving her a wink, making her smile.

With three people on the job, the cleaning up and putting things to rights was done in an hour and Annalise packed an overnight bag and followed Eva and Jim to Eva's house for the night.

Before leaving this time, she went through the entire house, checking every window and door to ensure it was locked. It wouldn't keep anyone from breaking a window to climb in, but at least she'd done her part to make it harder for them.

CHAPTER EIGHT

~

*M*ichael Granger woke up with a record-breaking hangover he thought could have been entered into the Guinness Book of World Records. Surely there must be a category for that, considering how many other ridiculous things they kept track of. He'd spent the previous night at his local bar drowning his sorrows about his current financial situation, losing count of how many beers he'd downed and proving once again it solved nothing. His problems were still waiting for him the next day. Shuffling his way into the bathroom, he removed the bottle of aspirin from the medicine cabinet and shook two into the palm of his hand. Considering, he shook one more out for good measure and walked back into the kitchen, got a glass from the cabinet, and poured himself a glass of water, chugging the contents down along with the aspirin.

"You really need to clean up this pig stye," he told himself as he looked around the room and the smell of rotting food filled his nose. The sink and countertop around it were filled with dirty dishes. The two pots on the stove contained the dried-up leavings of the soup and chili he'd heated up days before. On the kitchen table was a pizza box he thought might still have two slices of pizza from the night before. He wasn't above having cold pizza for breakfast even if it hadn't been refrigerated, but when he lifted the lid, the leftover slices were covered with ants. Disgusted, he picked up the box and threw it outside on the back deck. He would put it in the garbage can later, he promised himself. Michael hadn't always been this way about keeping his house clean, but the past two months had been difficult emotionally and physically. His live-in girlfriend of the last two years had left him, and business had been slow at the vinyl siding installation company where he worked, so his hours had been cut. He was making it, but just barely. He might not have enough money to pay the rent this month, which made his going out for a night of drinking even more of a mistake. Something his inner critic was scolding him about now. Ignoring it as much as possible, he set up his coffeemaker and poured himself a bowl of cereal to eat while he waited for it to finish. He wasn't sure his stomach would handle it, but taking the aspirin on an empty stomach wasn't the best idea either, so he decided he should at least try to eat. The bowl of cereal stayed down and, along with three cups of coffee, he was beginning to feel human again. He retrieved the newspaper from the front porch and returned to the kitchen to read while he finished the pot of coffee. A story about a woman who had a piece of a treasure map she'd inherited from her great-grandfather caught his attention. His interest was piqued even more when he read the backstory about how she had come into its possession. By the time he finished reading the story, his hangover was completely forgotten. The article mentioned it was a follow-up piece to a story The Bangor News had published about two teenagers finding a copper bottom boat in the Kenduskeag River and the skeleton that was beneath it with a bullet hole in its skull. Michael had missed seeing the earlier article.

Was it possible the letter in which his great-grandfather had written a deathbed confession admitting he'd killed one partner and wounded, probably killing the other, while looking for treasure really be true? It had been passed from father to son until he had been the most recent recipient who inherited the letter and two pieces of a treasure map from his father. He'd dismissed the confession as BS when his father had first shown it to him, but the newspaper article had mentioned the names Frank Abbott, John, and Harvey, which was his great-grandfather's name. It couldn't possibly be a coincidence that all three names matched the confession. And the copper bottom boat, he reminded himself. The pieces fit, but he wanted to read the letter again and compare it to the newspaper story. Retrieving the fireproof metal box from the shelf in his closet, he brought it to the kitchen where he'd left the newspaper. Inside, underneath his other important papers, he found the envelope, now yellow with age. Carefully removing the letter from its envelope, he opened it to find the two pieces of a hand drawn treasure map tucked inside. He placed them on the table and read the letter that had been written by his great-grandfather just before his death in 1966.

September 5, 1966

I've carried this secret with me for most of my life, but now that I am dying, I want to unburden myself and ask the Lord for forgiveness for what I did all those years ago. This is my confession for my sins.

In 1926, I won a treasure map in a poker game. I don't remember the name of the guy I won it from, but he claimed it had belonged to the

pirate Dixie Bull. I looked it up later in the
library and there really was a pirate by that name
here in Maine in the 1600s, so I thought it must
be true. I talked my friends, John Nelson and
Frank Abbott, into helping me find the treasure if
I would split it with them. We figured out where
we thought it would be after looking at maps from
back then and comparing them to the maps we had
in 1926. It turned out to be on the Kenduskeag
River once you've followed it up from where it
meets the Penobscot River in Bangor. Frank was the
one who had the idea of splitting up the map into
three pieces so no one could double-cross the others.
John thought that was a good idea, too, so I cut it
up and we each had a piece. John had a copper
bottom boat he'd made himself that he went in, and
Frank and I went in another boat. We wanted to
have one to put the gold in by itself and we'd come
back all together in the other one. The day we
decided to look started out sunny, so we didn't
think twice about going out, but it took us a lot
longer to get there than we'd thought, even using the
boat motors. We realized we couldn't go there and
back on the same day, so had a tent and supplies
with us to camp out for two or three days.

This is the part where I have to make my
confession. I don't know what came over me. Some
people call it gold fever and maybe that's what it

was. I don't know, but it doesn't matter. Whatever it was, I wish to God I'd never won that map. We had reached the part of the river where we'd have to pull the boats in and follow the map on land to where the treasure was buried. Frank was already out of our boat, and I was tying it up. John had pulled his boat in beside us and was tying that one up. I had meant it when I told them I would split the treasure with them but the more I thought about it, the more I wanted it all for myself. I'd won that map, so it should be mine. All the way up the river, I argued with myself. These were my friends and what I was thinking of doing wasn't right, but the fever was in me. I had brought a gun and convinced myself I only meant to use it to threaten them and take the treasure for myself, but I knew as soon as we landed on that shore that I was going to have to kill them if I wanted to pull it off. I shot John in the head, and it killed him instantly. Frank turned around as soon as he heard the shot and I'll never forget the look on his face. He couldn't believe I'd done it. He asked me, Harvey, what are you doing? He came at me and punched me, knocking me down. By the time I got up, he was running away. My first shot grazed his arm, but the next one got him in his side. I don't know to this day how he managed to get away, but he kept running into the woods and I couldn't see him well enough to shoot again. I thought I could catch up to him, so I took John's piece of the map out of his wallet before I started chasing Frank. It had taken us longer than we thought it would and the clouds had started coming in by then. One minute it was all sunshine and the next, the sky was almost dark as night, even though it was only late afternoon. I started out after Frank and was able to follow his trail at first because he was losing blood. I would have been able to catch him if it hadn't started raining. It was as though the heavens had opened up, the rain was coming down so heavy. I knew if I didn't go back, I would lose my way and as bad as Frank was wounded, he wasn't likely to make it far. I turned around and ran back to the river figuring I'd have to go back later to find his body. I dumped John's body into the bottom of his boat and wrapped some rope first around him and then the center seat so his body would stay with the boat. Then I tossed out the anchor so it would keep the boat hooked where it was. I had no idea if it would work, but I had gotten the idea to shoot a few holes in his boat so it would sink on top of him. I got in John's boat and rowed out, towing the other boat with me. Once I got out far enough that I thought the boat would be below the surface enough so nobody would see it, I decided to try to just turn the boat over and capsize it instead of shooting holes in it. I was already soaked to the skin, so I stood up, rocking the boat back and forth until I managed to tip it over and was able to jump out far enough away that I didn't get caught underneath it. The weight of the motor helped pull it down. Then I swam over to the other boat and rowed back to shore to wait out the storm. I was too exhausted by that point to try going back home until it stopped raining. It was dark by the time it did, but I knew I had to clear out of there and take my chances that Frank was dead and no one would figure out who killed him. I never saw him again, so I figure that's what happened. When I got back to Belfast, I told the cops we got caught in the storm and John's boat capsized with him and Frank in it. I said I tried getting back to help them but didn't make it in time. They'd already gone under, and their bodies never came up. I figured they were goners and had to come back to shore. After a few days, people stopped looking for them. Everyone figured the current had taken their bodies out to the ocean.

I never went looking for the treasure again. The madness that had taken over me went away and I realized just what I had done. There hasn't been a day since then that I haven't thought of them and *been sorry for what I did. I hope the Lord knows that and will forgive me now that I've confessed my sins to Him and to anyone who finds this letter to see.*

Harvey Granger

MICHAEL PLACED the letter and pieces of the map back into the envelope, convinced beyond any doubt that it was John Nelson whose body had been found with the copper bottom boat. Harvey had said he had never gone back for the treasure. Chances were it was still out there, and he was going to be the one who finally found it. He would need help, though, and he knew just who he could ask.

CHAPTER NINE

⁓

"*D*id you guys read these stories in The Bangor News?" Michael asked, and handed over the articles he'd torn out of the newspapers to Bill Robinson. "You need to read this one first, so when you're done, hand it over to Tim and then the second one when you're done with that."

Michael sat nervously as he waited for them both to finish reading.

"So?" Tim asked, shrugging his shoulders.

"I wanted you to read those first before I told you about something my father gave me that belonged to my great-grandfather, Harvey. You might get upset, but just remember, I had nothing to do with this and Harvey's dead now, so there's nothing anyone can do about it."

"Just say whatever it is," Bill said, frowning, and Michael could tell he was annoyed.

"It's about your great-grandfathers, too. Tim, I'm pretty sure the skeleton they found is your great-grandfather, John Nelson. And the guy named Frank Abbott was yours, Bill."

"Can't be. Our great-grandfathers drowned when they got caught out in the Gulf of Maine during a storm. They weren't anywhere near the Kenduskeag River," Tim disagreed.

"I'm telling you, it's them. My dad gave me this before he died," Michael said, taking the letter and pieces of the map out of the envelope he'd been holding and laid it on the table. "Read the letter. It's Harvey's confession about what really happened. The names match what that Annalise Jordan told the reporter. Frank Abbott was your great-grandfather and John was yours. The article says she doesn't know the last names, but it has to be them. And here's what clinches it. I've got the other two pieces of the map." He laid those on the table beside the letter.

Tim and Bill exchanged glances and then Bill took the letter. When he was done reading, he handed it over to Tim. When he was finished, Tim looked up at Michael, a shocked expression on his face.

"What the hell, Michael?"

"Don't be mad at me. It's ancient history and we can't bring them back. That's not why I'm telling you now, anyway. These are the other two pieces of the map." He slid them across the table, closer to Bill and Tim.

"Okay, it all seems to fit," Bill agreed after looking at them. "But what are you planning to do about it? Do you really think this woman will just hand over the one she has if we ask her real nice?"

"And even if she does, then what?" Tim followed up.

"We find the treasure. My great-grandfather never went back to find it and Frank Abbott couldn't have either. He died that same night."

"You're kidding, right? That treasure either wasn't ever there or it got dug up a long time ago. The map was probably completely bogus," Bill scoffed.

"It's worth at least looking, isn't it? We all could use the money." Michael used what he hoped would be the convincing argument.

Bill and Tim looked at each other, both knowing it was true.

"Ok. We try to get the other piece. How?"

"We find out where she lives. We know she's in Glen Lake from what it said in The Bangor News. You can find anybody these days just by putting in their name on the internet. We case her house and break in when she's gone. The article said she had it in a jewelry box she got from her father. We find that and figure out where we go from there."

Bill and Tim remained skeptical.

"We *need* the money," Michael repeated, more forcefully this time. "We break in when she's not home. No one gets hurt. I promise."

"One time. If it doesn't work, we bail and leave it at that. There are other ways to make money," Bill said after thinking it over.

"One time," Tim agreed, stating his terms as well.

"Okay, then," Michael said, smiling and feeling more optimistic about his future than he had in weeks.

They spent the next fifteen minutes on Michael's laptop looking up Annalise Jordan. When they found her name and that she lived in Glen Lake but no actual address, Tim agreed to front the money for a deeper dive into a search of her name and location.

"It's amazing what you can find out on the internet these days, isn't it?" Michael said, his mood becoming jubilant once they'd found what they needed. "We'll try tomorrow. Meet me here at nine o'clock."

CHAPTER TEN

≈

*I*t wasn't easy to be discreet about watching Annalise's house for a time when she wasn't home. She lived on one of the two major roads going through Glen Lake and being rural, they had only the shoulder to park the car since it would raise even more suspicions to be in a neighbor's driveway which was several hundred yards away on either side. They finally agreed they should park just beyond her house on the opposite side of the road where there was no house and a stand of woods where they could hide, concealed from anyone passing by. Bill and Tim had been unhappy about all the time they had taken already and were arguing with Michael that it was a waste of time and they should just give up.

"She's leaving," Michael announced. "Nobody's home at either of the neighbors' houses either. I say we try now."

He led the way, running across the street and down to Annalise's house, and then to the back of the house, with Bill and Tim behind him. Passing the window in the kitchen, which was too high to bother with, he went on to the remaining two and placing his hands on either side of his face, he peered in. The window screens made it more difficult, but fortunately, the curtains were sheer, and he could tell it was the dining room.

"You try the one on the end and I'll try this one," he told Bill.

He removed the screen, setting it down on the ground and tried pushing the bottom half of the window up. At first, it would only move a fraction, but while Bill was still struggling with the screen on the other window, he was able to lift it enough to reach inside and push from the bottom.

"I'm in. Forget that one and follow me."

Once inside, they quickly scanned the dining room. Finding nothing that resembled a man's jewelry box, they made their way into the room Annalise used for her Reiki sessions and then on to the living room.

"Go through the bookcases in case she hid it behind something," Michael directed.

They each picked a section and tossed books onto the floor. Tim finished his section first and after looking around the room, decided to look under the couch cushions. It seemed like an odd place to hide a jewelry box, but he reasoned it made it even more likely, at least while the owner was out of the house.

"What are you doing?" Bill asked him. "Who would put a jewelry box under their couch cushion?"

"You never know," Tim replied defensively.

"It's not here. Let's go upstairs and check the bedrooms," Michael said.

They pounded up the stairs and when they reached the top, each headed in a separate direction, almost as though they had already agreed which way to go. Michael was the one who found Annalise's bedroom. He rushed to the bureau when he spied a jewelry box on top of it and flung open the lid. Inside was what his ex-girlfriend had called costume jewelry. Pretty, but nothing of value from what he saw at first glance, and that wasn't what he was here for, anyway. He turned it over, shaking the contents onto the top of the bureau. Disappointed to find no map inside, he realized there must be another jewelry box. He went through her bureau drawers next, dumping the contents on the floor. Still finding nothing, he moved on to the closet. First, he pushed aside the clothes in case there might be a hidden safe, but no joy there either. On the shelf above the hanging rod were several purses. Grabbing one, he looked inside before tossing it on the floor and moving on to the next. All empty. He felt his temper rising. *It has to be here. She told that reporter she had it.* By now, Tim and Bill had finished looking through the other bedrooms and joined him.

"One more room to check," Michael told them, and walked into Annalise's sitting room, where his eyes were drawn to the wooden jewelry box sitting on a side table. He nearly ran over to it, knowing that had to be it. "I found it!" he announced, his voice rising with excitement. He picked up the box and opened the lid.

"What the hell is this?" he asked rhetorically when he discovered all that was inside were some tie clips and a pair of cuff links. He tossed them on the table and looked inside the box one more time in disbelief and disappointment.

"She must have taken it with her," he finally spoke, his voice registering the sense of defeat that matched the expression on his face. "We might as well go. We don't want to be here when she comes back."

Tim and Bill exchanged a glance, agreeing without speaking aloud to stay quiet. They followed Michael down the stairs and out the window they'd used to enter, not bothering to close it or replace the screen. Dejectedly, Michael walked around to the front of the house, looking in both directions before continuing to the road and his car. No one spoke as they all climbed in and drove away.

CHAPTER ELEVEN

~

The Cozy Quilts Club had gathered for their weekly meeting and potluck supper. With strawberry season in full swing, the challenge this week had been to include strawberries in every course. After their first meeting, the members had agreed that rather than leaving the courses to chance each week, they would choose from slips of paper placed in a basket, each having one of the four courses to be served written on it. Eva had groaned the week before when she had pulled the entrée slip from the basket.

"I can't wait to see what you came up with, Eva," Jennifer said when they had finished the strawberry bruschetta appetizer she had brought.

"You may all remember how much I groaned last week when I drew the lucky entrée slip," she said, using air quotes for lucky, eliciting chuckles from the others. "I shouldn't have been surprised you can find lots of recipes to choose from when you do an internet search. I ended up picking one for grilled chicken with strawberry avocado salsa. It should go nicely with the salad that Sarah brought."

"It's almost as though we planned it. Even though we didn't!" Sarah added. "It's a spinach strawberry salad with a poppy seed dressing."

"Sounds yummy. I thought about making strawberry short-cake for dessert, but decided it was too predictable, so I pulled out my ice cream maker and made strawberry ice cream instead," Annalise said.

"Strawberry ice cream is my favorite and homemade straw-berry ice cream is even better," Jennifer said.

While Eva grilled the chicken, they sat together in the screened three season room located near the grill and discussion turned to the break-in at Annalise's house.

"How are you doing?" Jennifer asked, a frown of concern on her face.

"I'm okay now. I was rattled when I saw what the intruder or intruders had done, but thank goodness Eva and Jim came over to be with me until Deputy Tremblay arrived. I still can't thank both of you enough for helping me put everything back in its place and suggesting I stay with you that night. I don't think I would have recovered as quickly otherwise."

"Was anything taken?" Sarah asked.

"No, and other than the mess they made, there wasn't any damage."

"Why do you think they broke in?" Jennifer asked.

"I don't have any way to prove it, but I'm convinced they came because of the story in The Bangor News about the treasure map. I haven't been able to form a clear picture in my head yet; it's still just a feeling that the past and the present are connected somehow."

"Are you worried that they'll try again? You know you're always welcome to stay with me if you're not comfortable being alone," Eva asked.

"I'm not sure… maybe… about the breaking in again part. And thank you for the offer. It's very much appreciated, but I should be okay."

"Have you thought about Jim's suggestion to have a security system installed? It might not be a bad idea with you being on your own," Eva suggested.

"You're probably right. It makes me angry I would have to do that, though. I've always felt safe in my home, and I'm well aware being stubborn about this isn't the smartest thing given what's happened."

"What's that saying about being smart or being right? It may not be exactly on point, but do you get the gist of what I mean?" Sarah asked.

"I do, and I'll give it more thought, ladies. I promise."

"Group hug," Jennifer said, arms outstretched as she went to Annalise. Eva and Sarah followed suit, and they all hugged.

Here we go again with another kumbaya moment. Eva heard Reuben's voice in her head and noticed him sitting on the floor facing them, giving what she thought of as his eyeroll expression. She gave him a warning glare, letting him know his comment was not appreciated. Taking the hint, he walked back to the living room.

"Okay, then, how about we move on to why we came tonight and start quilting?" Eva suggested.

"Good idea!" Annalise agreed, glad to have the conversation ended.

Everyone went to their sewing machines to work on their projects until Eva announced their meeting time was up.

"I could have kept right on sewing," Sarah said. "This has been such a great stress reliever for me to get out of the house and be with all of you. It's giving Ashley some much-needed alone time, too. With me working at home, that doesn't happen a lot."

Jennifer laughed at that. "I think David would agree with

Ashley. He's not exactly alone with two teenagers still at home, but more often than not, they're out with friends so he still gets a break."

"Only one more thing before we go," Eva said after everyone had packed up their projects and she brought out what they now referred to as the potluck basket. "We need a theme, and everyone needs to pick their course. I have to admit, it was interesting to come up with a strawberry main course, but my vote is for no strawberries next time."

"Agreed," Jennifer said. "The days are getting hotter. What if we make something cold for all the dishes?"

"That could be fun. I'm in," Annalise said.

Eva and Sarah both put a thumbs up.

"Okay, time to pick a slip," Eva said, holding the basket out for Annalise to choose, and then passed it to Sarah and Jennifer before taking the last slip for herself. "I now declare this week's meeting adjourned."

CHAPTER TWELVE

~

*O*nce home, Annalise thought about the suggestion of adding a home security system. She had to admit it made sense. Nothing had happened other than having to clean up a mess, but what if she had been home or came home before they left? Her intuition was practically shouting this wasn't the end of it and as long as she had the map piece, she would be in danger. There was nothing she could do about it tonight, but tomorrow she would call a security company and arrange to have a system installed. She felt a little better as she walked through the house, checking every door and window to make sure they were locked. If nothing else, it would mean she wouldn't have to do this every night or whenever she left the house.

She had slept most of the night, more peaceful than she had been since the break-in. Just as dawn was about to break, she woke with a start. She had been dreaming. In her dream, she was being held hostage by two men. She had the sense that they were younger, perhaps in their forties, but she couldn't see their faces because they were wearing ski masks. They had broken into her house and knocked her unconscious just as she was heading upstairs. When she awoke, she was tied to one of her dining room chairs and was sitting face to face with one of her captors.

Where's the map? he demanded as soon as she opened her eyes.

It's in the jewelry box, she answered.

You're lying! We already checked.

It has a secret compartment.

Go get the jewelry box he said to her other captor, and he left to go upstairs.

Your great-grandfather didn't have any right to keep the map. It belonged to mine.

CHAPTER THIRTEEN

⤳

That's when Annalise had woken up. She knew instantly that was what had been nagging at her. Her intuition was trying to tell her something more was going on. She remained in bed, struggling to get a handle on whether the dream had just been a warning or a premonition of something about to happen, but the sense of knowing which, warning or premonition, was eluding her. What did it mean when her captor said the map belonged to his great-grandfather? Was he somehow related to Frank Abbott? Or maybe to the man who had shot him? How could she find out? Would that help even if she did? All those thoughts were going through her mind, but there were no answers forthcoming. Giving up, she got out of bed and headed to the shower. Maybe once she had more time to think, the answers would come. One thing she did know, though, if she hadn't been sure about putting in a security system before, she definitely was now.

⤳

HER CALLS to security companies hadn't been as productive as she'd hoped. It would be at least a week before any of them had an opening to install the alarm system. She made the appointment and hoped nothing would happen in the meantime.

Out of nowhere, she heard a voice in her head: *Call Sarah and ask her to contact Frank Abbott. He can tell you their names.* After that settled into her consciousness and she chided herself for not thinking about Sarah's ability to communicate with the dead sooner, she accepted the advice and called her.

"Hi, Sarah. It's Annalise."

"Good morning! It's good to hear from you, but should I be asking if there's something I can do for you?"

"Hey, who's the psychic here?" Annalise teased.

"Definitely you, but you are giving off a vibe," Sarah replied.

"Your vibe radar is right. I'm calling to ask if you would be willing to try contacting Frank Abbott. He's the man who came to my great-grandparents and had the piece of the treasure map."

"Of course! Anything I can do to help. Do you have something in particular you want to know?"

"Yes. I'm hoping he can give me more information about his partners. Remember I said last night I had a feeling it was something more than just a random break-in?"

"Yes, I remember."

"I think it's connected somehow to their descendants." She went on to tell Sarah about her dream.

"That makes a lot of sense," Sarah replied once Annalise was finished. "When would be a good time for me to come? And when are you getting that security system installed?" she added.

"Can you come tonight after you're done working? To answer your other question, I've already made an appointment with a security company. They'll be here next week. That's the earliest any of the companies I called would be able to do it," she said, anticipating Sarah's next question.

"I'm glad to hear you made the appointment and will cross my fingers nothing happens in the meantime. Would it be too late to come around seven or seven-thirty? That would give Ashley and me time to have dinner first."

"That would be fine. I'll see you then."

CHAPTER FOURTEEN

~

A sense of anticipation and relief washed over Annalise when the doorbell rang announcing Sarah's arrival. She had been looking forward to this all day, and it had occupied nearly every thought.

"Please come in," she said, closing the door behind Sarah and then giving her a hug. "I can't tell you how much this means to me."

"I hope I don't disappoint you. It might not work if he doesn't want to be contacted," Sarah cautioned.

"Of course. If it doesn't happen, it doesn't happen. All we can do is try. Can I bring you something to drink first?"

"A glass of water would be good."

Annalise gave her a tour of the downstairs on their way to the kitchen.

"It's a beautiful home. Do you know which room Frank Abbott...?" she paused for Annalise's confirmation of his name, "was in when he passed?"

"The story I heard was that he was in the living room."

"Let's go in there and see what happens."

Annalise led the way and sat in one of the chairs, and Sarah sat in the other.

"I am here to speak with the spirit of Frank Abbott. I have questions about the people you were with just before you died, if you are willing to tell me." She then closed her eyes. They sat quietly for several minutes before Sarah opened her eyes and spoke, looking at the couch. Annalise was not aware of anything having changed, but realized Sarah must be seeing Frank's ghost.

"Hello, Frank. Thank you for coming. This is my friend Annalise," she said, looking over at Annalise. "It was her great-grandparents who lived in this house and helped you after you were shot."

"His name was Frank, too. That's what his wife, Nellie, told me, although she called him Franklin. I was grateful for their kindness. I know they weren't able to save me, but I'd lost too much blood by the time I got to their house. They did their best."

"It's our understanding that your friends' names were Harvey and John, but is there anything else you can tell me about them? Their last names?"

"I thought Harvey was our friend, but when it happened, I didn't think he was much of one after all," Frank said. "I realize now from being on this side that he was not in his right mind. The gold fever got him."

"Can you tell me more about what happened? We have the information that he shot and killed your other friend before he shot you. The story you told Nellie and Franklin was passed down through the generations, but no one knows what their last names were or where you all came from. Did you have wives or children?"

"We were all married. My wife's name was June, and we had a daughter named Marian. We lived in Belfast. So did Harvey and John. Harvey's last name was Granger. He had a wife named Cynthia and two sons. The older one was named Aaron and the other one was Elliott. John Nelson's wife was Martha, and they had a boy named Lucas. Did our wives find out what happened to me and John?" he asked, sadness in his voice.

"I don't think they ever did, Frank. John's body wasn't found until just a couple weeks ago and Nellie and Franklin didn't know anything about where you were from to tell the police when they came for your body. Things were different back then, and it was much more difficult to track people down. As far as Annalise knows, Harvey never confessed to what he'd done, so the police didn't have any idea he was the one responsible." She turned to Annalise. "Frank is asking if anyone ever found out what happened to him and John. Is what I told him accurate?"

"My grandparents never said otherwise, so I think what you told him is true. Did he tell you who the others were?"

"Yes, their names were Harvey Granger and John Nelson. I'll tell you the rest when we're done. Is there anything else you wanted me to ask Frank?"

"Does he know if the break-in is connected?"

"Frank, after John's body was found, a story about it was printed in The Bangor News. When Annalise read about the copper bottom boat, she remembered the story you told her grandparents, which was passed down in her family along with the piece of the map you had. She got in touch with the newspaper and told them your story and that she has the piece of the treasure map you had with you. Annalise's house was broken into after the story was printed in the paper, and she thinks it might be connected. Is there any way you would know if that is true?"

"She shouldn't have that. That map is cursed and will only lead to more death. Tell her to get rid of it!"

Sarah could tell that Frank was agitated, and she turned immediately to Annalise.

"Frank is very concerned for you. He wants you to get rid of the map. He's afraid it will lead to more death."

Annalise thought for a moment and then nodded her head. "Tell him I will. If we can find Harvey Granger's descendants, I'll give it to them. My intuition is telling me he kept the other pieces of the map and, just like my grandparents passed along Frank's story, I think Harvey did the same for his side of it."

Sarah turned back to Frank and repeated what Annalise had told her. Frank didn't appear completely convinced, but at last nodded his head as though making up his mind it would be okay.

"It's probably the only thing that can be done. Harvey always wanted to have it all. If he never got his way then, maybe it will be enough that his family will have it now. If they're anything like he was, they won't give up until they do. Throwing it away wouldn't break the curse."

Sarah turned to Annalise. "Frank thinks that's the best thing to do, too." She chose not to pass along the rest of his warning and hoped she wasn't making a mistake. "Can I tell him it's okay to go now?"

"I can't think of anything else. Do you think what he told you will be enough to find them?"

"I think so. We have last names and where they were living. It should be enough to find them with the research methods we have available now."

"Please thank him for me."

"Annalise asked me to thank you and so do I. We don't have any other questions if you would like to go now."

"If I have anyone left in my family, will you tell them what happened to me and how sorry I am that I left them like I did? The gold fever took over me a little bit, too. I only wanted to make things better. I thought once I had my share of that treasure, everything would be okay, and I could give June the house I always promised her we'd have. I never meant for it to turn out the way it did."

"We're sorry for what happened to you, Frank. If there's any way we can let your family know what happened, we will. I promise."

"Thank you. I'm going to go now."

With that, his image faded.

"He's gone," Sarah said, turning to Annalise.

"Do you really think we can find out who their descendants are?"

"I can't say absolutely, but we've got a lot better chance than they did in 1926. I'll start looking as soon as I'm back home. My curiosity is piqued, and I want to find out almost as much as you do. The sooner we find them, the sooner you can give back the map and be safe."

"I hope so, too. If I can do anything to help on my end, let me know."

"I will. I should probably be going, but I'll be in touch as soon as I find anything."

Annalise closed the door behind Sarah and locked it. Once again, she went through the house checking every door and window, thinking to herself that the installation of the security system couldn't come soon enough.

CHAPTER FIFTEEN

~

*A*nnalise had finished a Reiki session two days later, when she received a call from Sarah.

"I got lucky! Between census records and some research sources that shall remain anonymous, I've been able to find information on all three of them."

"That's amazing! I wasn't expecting you to find anything so soon."

"Insert the deity of your choice to bless the internet! I was planning to take this afternoon off, so I can bring over what I've learned if you're going to be home."

"Eva and I are meeting for lunch at twelve-thirty at The Checkout Diner. Why don't you join us? My treat as a thank you for helping me out. I'm sure Eva would love to hear more of the story, too."

"That sounds great. I'll see you there."

Annalise had already arrived and taken a seat facing the entrance in one of the booths when Sarah and Eva come through the door. She waved to catch their attention, and they joined her, sitting opposite from her.

"I had told Eva about your conversation with Frank, so she's up to speed."

"Oh, good. We got here at the same time, so haven't had time to say more than hello."

They paused their conversation as they perused the menus. Once Betty Jones brought them water and took their lunch orders, Sarah placed the folder she'd brought with her on the table.

"It was a lot easier than I'd thought it would be, but having the complete names Frank gave and that they lived in Belfast really helped. I also found a newspaper story from shortly after Frank came to your great-grandparent's house. Apparently, Harvey Granger... he's the one Frank told them had shot him and John Nelson... told everyone they had drowned. He claimed John and Frank were in the same boat and he was in the other one. He used the storm as an excuse to say their boat capsized and he wasn't able to rescue them before they drowned. The authorities must have believed him, even though the bodies never resurfaced anywhere. From what I read, that would be possible, especially if they were caught in a current and went out to the ocean. The newspaper article mentioned their widows' names and I found obituaries for them that matched with the names Frank gave me. Using the names in those I was able to check more census records and genealogical sites to keep going with their histories. It helped that they all stayed in the area."

She paused to let Betty give them their orders.

"How are you doing, Annalise? I heard about the break-in at your house. Was anything stolen?" Betty asked.

Annalise looked taken aback. "I'm surprised you know about that. It wasn't reported in the paper."

"It's a small town. News travels fast," Betty said, giving her a wink.

"To answer your question, though, I was really lucky nothing was stolen and I didn't come home while the burglar was still in the house."

"That would have been terrible! I'm so glad it turned out okay, all things considered," she said, giving Annalise a pat on the shoulder before returning to the counter where a man was seated.

Annalise hadn't been aware of him when she'd first come in, but something caught her attention now. It was a feeling more than anything physical about him, but before she could dig deeper, Sarah had begun talking again and she turned her attention back to her.

"I was able to trace each of their lines to the most current descendants. Their names are Michael Granger, Timothy Nelson, and William Robinson. Robinson is Frank Abbott's descendant. Remember, he had a daughter named Marian? She married into the Robinson family. It seems a little strange, but in Frank's family each generation only had one child, a male, until ending up with William. I was even able to find high school yearbook pictures that show Michael, Timothy who goes by Tim, and William who goes by Bill, all together. Sort of a BFF thing, and Michael and Bill work for the same siding company. That's one of those don't ask, don't tell resources I mentioned."

"This is all fascinating!" Eva said once Sarah had finished. "I can't believe you were able to piece this all together."

"It helps that there's so much interest in genealogy now that it's easy for people to have their DNA tested. Plus all the genealogical sites you can access on the internet these days."

"And your secret sources," Annalise smiled.

"And those," Sarah agreed, returning her smile.

Betty returned with their orders and the conversation turned to how they were each progressing with their quilt projects.

"I should probably head back home. I promised Ashley we

would spend some time together this afternoon and she should be getting home soon," Sarah said when she had finished her lunch.

"I need to go home, too. My cousin, Sharon Peterson, is back from Arizona and is coming over to visit in about an hour. I should say Sharon Ramos," Annalise corrected herself. "I haven't quite gotten used to that, as she just got married again this past January. Anyway, she's also a quilter, and we have been meaning to get together. I've told her a little about the Cozy Quilts Club and she wanted to see the project I'm working on this month."

"You should invite her to one of our meetings," Eva suggested. "We'd love to have another quilter join us."

"Yes, please ask her to come," Sarah said.

"I'll do that!"

As Annalise was getting out of the booth, her attention was drawn once again to the man at the counter paying his bill. He turned in her direction and their eyes met. An image of him picking up her jewelry box flashed in her brain. Her eyes widened, but she was able to maintain her composure. He turned back to take his change and then walked out.

"The man who just left was the person who broke into my house," Annalise said, keeping her voice low so only Eva and Sarah would hear.

"What?!" Eva exclaimed, turning around to look out the window, but he was already gone.

"Are you sure?" Sarah asked.

"I had a vision of him holding the jewelry box where I keep the map," Annalise said.

"Whoa! I wonder what he was doing here. Will you be okay going home?"

"I'll go with you," Eva said. "I can stay at least until your cousin gets there so you won't be alone. Maybe I should call Jim, too."

Annalise was about to tell her it wasn't necessary, but reconsidered.

"I think that's a good idea. If he's following me or thinking about coming back to the house, it might discourage him with other cars in my driveway."

"I'll call Jim to ask if he can meet us at your house. Let's leave now and I'll follow you, so we will arrive at the same time."

They gave Sarah a hug and after Eva had spoken to Jim and he'd agreed to meet them at Annalise's house, they each got in their cars and headed in that direction. Annalise was relieved to see Jim had arrived before them when she pulled into her driveway.

"Thank you for coming, Jim."

"There's my knight in shining armor," Eva teased as she gave him a kiss on the cheek.

"I'm glad I could help. What's this Eva told me about you recognizing the person who broke into your house when you were at the diner?"

"This is going to be another one of those woo woo situations, Jim. I'm not going to be able to report to the police I had a vision of the guy holding my jewelry box. I can't imagine they'd even let me work with a sketch artist based on that."

"You're right about that. Have you got your security system installed yet?"

"They're coming next week. My cousin will be here soon and with so many cars in the driveway, I'm hoping even if he did follow me here, he'll drive away."

"Did you happen to see what kind of car he is driving?"

"No. None of us did. He must have parked on the other side of the building and left in the opposite direction from where we'd be able to see him. I think he knew as soon as our eyes met that I recognized him. It wasn't just me that got freaked out. Let's go inside while we wait for Sharon."

CHAPTER SIXTEEN

~

*M*ichael Granger's hands were shaking as he left the diner. He had driven by Annalise Jordan's house earlier, but kept going when he saw her car in the driveway. It was lunchtime, and he remembered seeing a diner in town from one of his previous visits. He was hungry, so thought he might as well go eat and then come back later. Maybe she'd be gone by then. He hadn't paid much attention when the women had come into the diner after him, but his ears had perked up when one of them was talking about Harvey Granger, Frank Abbott, and John Nelson. He couldn't hear much more of what she was saying because she was speaking quietly, but there was no way it was a coincidence. When the waitress asked the one who was facing him about the break-in at her house, that was the clincher. He avoided looking in their direction while he finished his lunch so he wouldn't attract their attention, but he was able to sneak a look at them in the mirror along the back wall facing him. He paid more attention to the one facing him who had to be Annalise Jordan, since that was the one the waitress was talking to about the break-in. Michael hadn't meant to, but as he was leaving, he looked in her direction and their eyes had met. The expression on her face told him she knew who he was. *How could she possibly know that?* he argued with himself. *We weren't there when she got back that day, so there's no way she would have seen us.* Still, he was convinced with a certainty he couldn't explain that she recognized him. He'd planned to go back by her house one more time, but he was too shaken and instead, he went back to his house in Belfast.

CHAPTER SEVENTEEN

~

*S*haron Peterson Ramos arrived at Annalise's house, and after making introductions, Eva and Jim took their leave. Annalise had debated telling Sharon why they were there, but in the end, decided she could share what had happened, even about her vision of the burglar. Sharon was open to believing paranormal abilities were true and accepted Annalise's psychic visions as not only possible, but probable. There had been many incidents Sharon knew about over the years which had proven their validity. Annalise believed Sharon might have skills of her own, too, even though she wasn't aware of them on a conscious level.

"Why do I have the feeling there's more to the story of why your friends were here?" she asked, affirming Annalise's thoughts on that score.

"You remember I told you about the break-in at my house?"

Sharon nodded, "Of course."

"While Eva and I were having lunch at The Checkout Diner along with our friend, Sarah, who is part of the Cozy Quilts

Club, a man was seated at the counter and when we saw each other, I had a vision of him holding my dad's jewelry box. I'm convinced it's what the break-in had to be about since nothing was stolen and it was right after the story in The Bangor News."

Sharon gasped. "Do you think he was here to try again?"

"It's a definite possibility. I could tell he was sure I recognized him even though we've never seen each other before. He left so quickly we never saw what kind of car he was driving or what direction he took. Eva thought she and Jim should come to wait with me until you got here. Our thinking was that he would move on if he saw a lot of cars in the driveway."

"Good thinking. But what happens after I leave? Should you come home with me tonight?"

"No, I don't feel his presence or feel threatened in any way. I think he left town once he knew I'd seen him."

Sharon didn't look convinced, but had known Annalise long enough to realize there was no point arguing, and when she was that sure about something, it was usually true.

"I'll trust you on this, but if you change your mind, you let me know."

"I will. I promise," she added, seeing the look on Sharon's face.

"Okay. Now tell me about this quilting club of yours and I'm dying to see the project you're working on."

"We've been meeting for a little over a month now, but we met at Quilting Essentials when we took a free-motion quilting course. Along with Eva and Sarah, who I just had lunch with, there's one more member, Jennifer Ryder. All of us except for Sarah live in Glen Lake but she lives in Bangor, so is just next to us. We hit it off at the course and decided we wanted to keep meeting and that's when we formed the Cozy Quilts Club. It's been such a wonderful experience for me. I've felt more centered and connected ever since. Even though it's been thirty years since Peter died, I haven't had friends who I've been this close to other than you. It may sound like hyperbole, but I really do feel like it's changed my life. It's filled a hole I wasn't even aware was there. I think I'd felt that way for so long that it had become my new normal."

Sharon nodded her head. "I know exactly what you mean. After Tom died, I felt so empty. Thankfully, I didn't have to wait thirty years for that to change. Spending half of my time in Arizona has been a big part of that, but having Joseph in my life is what filled that void that Tom's death had created."

"I'm so happy for you. I think Joseph is a dream come true."

"More than you know... although on second thought, maybe you do," Sharon said, as much a question as a statement. She hadn't told Annalise about the vivid dreams that had begun shortly after her arrival in Arizona for her first winter as a snowbird. There was, of course, no way she could prove it, but she believed the dreams had been memories of a past life she had shared with Joseph. He really was her dream come true.

"Just a guess," Annalise said with a smile. "Maybe someday you'll tell me about it."

"Remind me to bring you the dream journal I kept when I was in Arizona. That will explain it all."

"I can't wait to read it."

"So, tell me about this project you're working on," Sharon said, to change the subject.

"It's a pattern called Treasure Box that is on the Classic Quilts site. I found it doing a Google search after the news story about the copper bottom boat being found and remembering about the piece of the treasure map. It seemed like a fun way to tie it into the quilting and is a pattern that's adaptable to make in different sizes so we're all making different versions. I'm making mine as a throw. Wait here and I'll bring down what I've got done so far to show you."

They spent the rest of the afternoon exchanging ideas about

quilting and, by the time Sharon was ready to leave, Annalise felt much better.

"Are you sure you'll be okay, Lise? It wouldn't be any trouble at all for you to stay the night with Joseph and me."

"No, I don't feel the least bit anxious that he's still here in town or he'll come back." *Tonight, anyway,* the thought popped into her head, but she kept it to herself.

"Okay, but if you change your mind, just give me a call. The guest room is already set up, so it's no bother at all."

"I promise," Annalise said in her most convincing tone. "And please think about joining us at the next Cozy Quilts Club meeting."

"I just might do that. It sounds like it would be fun."

As soon as Sharon had turned out of the driveway, Annalise closed the door and repeated her new routine of going through the house to make sure the windows and doors were locked. She had been telling the truth about her intuition the burglar wouldn't return tonight, but better safe than sorry.

CHAPTER EIGHTEEN

~

*A*nnalise arrived at the next Cozy Quilts Club meeting with Sharon in tow.

"Look who the cat dragged in," she said to Eva when she opened the door.

Did she really say what I think she did? Reuben asked indignantly from his perch in the bay window.

"Don't get your fur in a twist, Reuben. It's just an expression," Eva said, turning in his direction.

Annalise laughed, and Sharon looked questioningly between the two women, waiting for an explanation.

"I haven't told her yet," she said to Eva. "I didn't want to do that without your permission, but Sharon is a believer in the woo woo, so no judgment."

"I'm able to communicate with animals," Eva explained to Sharon. "Reuben took offense at Annalise's cat dragging comment. He can be a little testy at times."

"He's such a handsome guy," Sharon said, taking a closer

look at Reuben. "He must be a Maine coon cat, judging from his size."

"Yes, he is. Are you a cat person?"

"I am, but unfortunately, I'm not able to have one now that I'm going back and forth between Maine and Arizona."

"That makes sense," Eva agreed. "I'm sorry, come in, come in. I didn't mean to keep you standing here in the doorway. We can put the food in the kitchen while we wait for Jennifer and Sarah to get here."

Jennifer is here, Reuben announced.

"Reuben just let me know Jennifer is here. Annalise, why don't you take Sharon into the kitchen, and I'll join you once Jennifer comes in."

Sarah arrived shortly after, and they all gathered in the kitchen. Annalise introduced Sharon to Jennifer and Sarah. "I hope you don't mind that I asked Sharon to join us. She's a quilter, too, and is only here until this fall, but I thought she'd be a nice addition to the group."

"Of course not! The more the merrier," Jennifer said, giving Sharon a warm smile.

"I don't have any problem with it either," Sarah said.

"Perfect! Now that that's settled, let's eat and then start on our projects. Annalise, did you fill Jennifer in about Sarah's conversation with Frank Abbott and the genealogy research?" Eva asked as she retrieved the food everyone had brought for the potluck.

"Not yet. Sharon knows some of this, but I'm okay with telling her all of what we learned if Sarah is okay with revealing how she spoke with Frank. You can trust Sharon. She has a very open mind and knows I'm a psychic and Eva is an animal whisperer," she said for Sarah and Jennifer's benefit.

"Your word is good enough for me," Sarah said and began her recitation of the contact she'd made with Frank and her genealogy research.

"That's amazing!" Sharon said when Sarah had finished. "I can't help thinking this is more than just coincidence. Have you thought about asking the police to become involved?"

"That's the downside of having these abilities. Even when we have information that would be valuable to the police, we can't just walk into the police station and make a report," Jennifer said. "There's got to be something we can do, though. We came up with a plan to catch Aunt Sadie's killer. We'll figure one out for this, too."

"Jennifer's great-aunt Sadie was murdered last month," Annalise explained to Sharon. "The police had run out of leads, but we came up with ideas to help them out. Sarah contacted Sadie and learned some of what had happened and then Eva spoke with Sadie's dog, Boscoe, who was able to tell her who the killer was. We tricked him into making a confession that we recorded on our phones and got his DNA on a glass he'd used when we offered him lemonade, and with Jim's help, we took that to the detectives investigating the case. They were desperate enough at that point to follow up, and not long afterwards, they had enough evidence to arrest the killer."

"That must have been an interesting conversation with the detectives."

"It certainly was. I was scared to death they'd think I was a kook and disregard everything, but having Jim with me gave me some credibility. And the rest is history," Jennifer said.

"For now, there's not much more we can do but wait to see if they try again. Hopefully by then I'll have the security system installed and it will scare them away."

"Fingers crossed," Eva agreed, holding up both hands with her fingers crossed.

"I've known about Annalise's ability since we were children, but I'm fascinated that all of you have your own unique skills. Did you realize you had them from the time you were a child, too?" Sharon asked.

"I did and thought everyone else could talk to animals, but my parents and other kids disabused me of that notion. It didn't take very long for me to realize they thought I was either making it up or was just weird. It's been such a relief to be with people who accept me for who I really am and I don't have to hide it anymore. At least with them."

"That's pretty much the same for me," Sarah said.

"It wasn't until I was in my late teens that I had my first experience," Jennifer said. "It was after my grandmother died and I was given a bracelet that had belonged to her. She knew I loved it and made sure it would be given to me after she was gone. When I put it on the first time, I had this image pop into my head of my grandmother when she was a teenager, and my grandfather was putting it on her wrist. I had no doubt it was them because there were pictures of them at that age in the family photo albums. He's the one who gave it to her, but I didn't know that then. I asked my mom if she knew anything about how Grandma got the bracelet, and she told me it was my granddad who had given it to her when they were dating in high school. I didn't say anything about what I'd seen. I guess somehow, I realized I'd be ridiculed if I did. Since then, I've had other experiences. The most recent one was when I was wearing a ring my Aunt Sadie left me and I saw what happened the night she was killed. It was as though I was looking through her eyes and saw Stephen Hill," Jennifer said, and her voice caught.

"Thank you all for trusting me enough to share this with me," Sharon said when they had finished.

"On that note, why don't we head to the sewing room and work on our projects? Annalise told me she's shown you the quilt block, Sharon, and I noticed you brought your machine and fabric. If you'll be coming to more of our meetings, and I hope you do; I'd like to nominate you as an honorary member of the Cozy Quilts Club."

"I second that!" Sarah said.

Annalise and Jennifer added their approvals.

"You are now officially one of us," Eva told Sharon. "We'll fill you in on how the potluck works, too, but for now, let's start sewing, ladies!"

CHAPTER NINETEEN

~

*B*y the time Michael got back to his house, he had regained his composure, but now had a sense of urgency about getting the last piece of the map. Somehow those women knew more about the map and who might have the other pieces than they should. Even worse was that Annalise Jordan recognized his face. It was just a matter of time before she connected his name to his face. He didn't know how he knew that, but he did.

"Bill. It's Mike. I need you to come over. We've got to talk about the map."

"I thought we agreed to give that up."

"I've changed my mind. I'm going to call Tim and have him meet us in half an hour. If you want in, be here. Otherwise, we'll split the treasure two ways instead of three."

There was a moment's hesitation before Bill replied that he would come.

"One down, one to go," Michael said to himself as he made the call to Tim.

"Tim, Bill's coming over in half an hour. We need to talk about how we're going to go after that third piece of the map."

"What? When did we change our minds about letting that go?"

"Since this afternoon. Are you in?"

"Fine. I'll see you in half an hour."

Michael looked around his house. It was filthy. A new batch of dirty dishes and takeout containers littered the kitchen and living room. The depression that had been creeping into nearly every waking moment of his life lately dug in even deeper. They had cut his hours even more, and his bank account was getting dangerously close to being overdrawn. He needed a break, and finding the treasure could solve everything. The guys wouldn't care about the mess, but he started cleaning up anyway. If nothing else, it gave him something to do while he waited for them and time to think of a plan. He felt a glimmer of hope as it came together. Now he just needed to convince Bill and Tim it would work.

Bill arrived first, with Tim following on his heels two minutes later.

"Did you make up with Kathie?" Bill asked, looking around at the apartment which was cleaner than at his last visit.

Michael snorted. "Not likely. She's gone for good. I can clean up after myself when I want to. I just hadn't been wanting to. Today I did. What's the big deal?"

"Hey, man, Bill didn't mean anything by it. The place looks nice. We haven't seen it like this for a while. That's all," Tim, always the peacemaker of the group, said, trying to take the tension down a notch.

"What he said," Bill agreed.

Michael relaxed, realizing he'd overreacted, but bringing up Kathie had struck a nerve.

"Yeah. Sorry. I've just been stressed out lately and that hit me the wrong way."

"No worries. What did you want to talk to us about?" Bill asked.

"I went up to Glen Lake this morning to check out Annalise Jordan's house again, but she was home. It was lunchtime, so I went to that diner, planning to go back by her house after I was done. I was sitting at the lunch counter when I overheard three women in one of the booths mention the names Granger, Nelson, and Abbott." He let that hang in the air to see if they caught on.

Bill was the first to realize its significance.

"Those are our great-grandparents' names. The ones who had the treasure map in the first place."

"Exactly. And then the waitress went over to their booth and asked one of them about the break-in at her house. That's when I realized she had to be Annalise Jordan. There's a mirror on the wall that faces the counter, so I was able to get a good look at her without turning around in case she caught me looking."

"And?" Tim asked.

"I couldn't hear anything else about what they were talking about, but I thought I heard them say our names. They've been doing some sort of genealogy thing."

Bill's face registered alarm, but Tim still hadn't picked up on the significance.

"So, now they know who had the map in the first place and that we're related. But there's no way they can connect us to the break-in, and we didn't find the other piece of the map, anyway," Bill reasoned.

"Yeah, but that piece belongs to us. It's the last thing we need so we can find the treasure. And we need to do it now," Michael said.

"What's the hurry? Wouldn't it be better to let things quiet down, and everybody forgets about it?" Tim asked.

"I don't have time for that," Michael said, his voice rising.

"If they keep digging, they might be able to put it together. Who else would have a motive?" Bill asked.

"Exactly. We might as well just draw a target on our backs," Tim agreed.

"Or we are in and out and make sure we don't leave any trace while she still has the other piece. What is she going to do? Tell the cops our great-grandfathers had the map back in 1926 because of some story she had been told? Even if she did, how could they prove it was us?" Michael realized it was best not to tell them what had happened when he and Annalise had looked at each other. If they were resisting already, it would have sealed the deal.

Bill and Tim still looked unconvinced.

"I don't know, man. It sounds too risky," Bill finally broke the silence.

"I'm with Bill. The treasure might not even be there. And then if we get caught, we'd be even worse off than we are now," Tim said.

Michael had to hold himself in check not to punch a hole in a wall. He had thought they would see his point and be on board. He didn't have any argument to come back with for their reasoning.

"Fine. You're probably right. I got my hopes up thinking it would solve everything if we could just get that last piece."

"It's too risky," Bill said.

"Yeah. I hadn't thought it through."

"Don't worry, Mike. It's tough right now, but it will get better," Tim said, trying to reassure him.

"Sorry I wasted your time."

Bill gave Michael's shoulder a friendly slap. "Don't worry about it. Tim's right. Things are going to get better. They couldn't get much worse, right?" he said with a smile.

"How about we go for a beer? My treat," Tim said, hoping to change the mood.

"Sure. Sounds good, especially the part about you treating," Michael replied, forcing a smile on his face. Inside, he was seething. He was determined to find a way to get that map, with or without them, and was willing to take the risk if it meant getting what he wanted.

CHAPTER TWENTY

∼

*M*ichael was still thinking about the map days later when he got a call from Tim. He had recently moved to an apartment in Bangor to be closer to his new job.

"Would you like to come check out my new apartment? Bill's out of town this week, but you and I can hang. There's a BBQ grill out back for everyone in the apartment building to use. I could grill some burgers."

This could be your chance to try again. Tim has always been easier to convince to do things. With Bill away, you might be able to talk him into coming with you to find the last piece of the map.

The voice in his head he'd been hearing for the past week was nagging at him again to keep looking for the treasure. It was the reason he had gone back to Annalise Jordan's house without Bill and Tim.

"Thanks, buddy. That sounds great. I can be there in about an hour."

"Great! See you soon."

On his way out, he thought of the gun given to him by his father along with the letter Harvey had written. It was the voice in his head again, telling him to retrieve it from the closet where he kept it on the overhead shelf. *I'll put it in the glove compartment.* He had no idea why he might need the gun, but he found himself unable to refuse what the voice was telling... no, *demanding* him to do.

"Come in," Tim said, opening the door for Michael. "The burgers are ready to put on the grill. Do you want to come out with me or stay here in the living room? The Sox are playing if you want to watch the TV while you wait."

"I'll come out with you. I'm not much of a baseball fan anymore."

"Whatever. Grab yourself a beer and one for me, will you? I'll take the burgers and buns."

Michael did as asked and followed Tim outside. He hadn't come up with an actual plan for how to convince Tim to go with him, but thought he could talk him into it if he played the sympathy card. It wasn't a lie, really. Things were desperate for him financially. After a few minutes of small talk, he began his pitch.

"I've been thinking more about the map," he began, but Tim interrupted him before he could finish.

"Not that again. Mikey, it's not a good idea. You remember what Bill said."

"Bill is scared of his own shadow. There's no way anyone can connect the dots to us. If the cops do come around, we'll alibi each other. We can wear gloves so we won't leave any fingerprints. Besides, you know cops don't do much when it comes to burglaries, and it's not like we're going to sell the map to have somebody else rat us out. I promise you; no one will get hurt. We'll make sure the Jordan woman is not in the house. You can even stay outside and keep watch while I go in so you're not the one stealing it. That way, we can make sure we both get away if she comes back early. We'll go in the back like we did before so no one can see us."

Tim didn't answer right away and Michael worried he was going to turn him down, so he played his trump card.

"I really need the money from the treasure, Tim. I'm broke. I'm not even going to be able to make the rent this month. You know Bill and I got laid off last week, don't you?"

"Yeah, he told me that's why he was going down to Massachusetts. He got a lead on a job down there."

"We need to do this as soon as possible. We can't wait for him to come back, and you know Bill. He'll try to talk us out of it again," Michael cajoled Tim. "We can split the money with him afterwards," he added, hoping that would win his case.

Tim put the cooked burgers and buns on the plates and nodded his head to Michael. "Open the door for me. My hands are full. Let me think about this for a minute."

Michael led the way, his hopes rising that he might have persuaded Tim. He let the subject drop while they ate their burgers, giving Tim the time he'd requested. They talked about the new apartment, Tim's new job, and crap Michael didn't give a damn about; everything except getting the map, and Michael felt his temper bubbling to the surface. When Tim still hadn't answered after they'd finished eating and was cleaning up the dishes instead, the voice began pushing him again. *Stop being such a coward. Take charge and make him help you.*

"Well, what do you think? Are you with me?"

"No one will get hurt?"

"I promise."

"Alright. I guess it's not a big deal if we can pull it off like you said. If we alibi each other, and stick to it no matter what, they've got no case. And if I stay outside, there's no chance there'd be any evidence I was there," he said, more to himself than to Michael. Michael could tell Tim was talking himself into going along with the plan and he should stay quiet. He didn't want to say anything to make him change his mind. "Okay, I'll help," Tim said at last.

"That's great, Tim. I promise you won't regret it."

"On one condition. I want one of the pieces of the map."

CHAPTER TWENTY-ONE

~

*M*ichael was stunned, but what did he have to lose? He needed all three pieces, but he could take it back later. After they had turned him down earlier, he'd made up his mind he would go to Jordan's house for the missing piece of the map, find the treasure, and then take it for himself. *Why should they have any of it, anyway? It was his great-grandfather who had won it in the poker game. Why had he even bothered with Frank Abbott and John Nelson?* Having Tim as his lookout just like he'd told him would make it easier, but after that…

He didn't realize he hadn't answered Tim yet about the map, and Tim was looking suspiciously at him.

"Sure, sure. They're in my glove box. I'll go get one of them for you now."

He walked down the street to the spot where he had parked his car and looked around to make sure no one was watching before tucking the gun in the back of his jeans underneath his shirt. The presence he'd felt telling him to take the gun was back again, nudging him. *Give him one of the pieces, but don't let him keep it no matter what. It's your birthright.*

Trancelike, he walked back into the house with the piece of the map. He realized he would have to at least show it to Tim, but he would obey the voice. *I won't let him keep it. I don't have any choice,* he told himself.

"Here you go," he said, holding it out to Tim, who studied it before folding it up again and pulled out his wallet placing it inside. Tim looked up to find Michael pointing a gun at him, and his face had changed. He didn't look like himself. It was as though he was a different version of himself, similar but not the same.

"Mike, what is wrong with you? Put the gun away before somebody gets hu…"

The sound of the gun discharging rang in Tim's ears, and he looked down to see his white tee-shirt turning red, and then everything went black.

CHAPTER TWENTY-TWO

~

*A*s soon as Tim's body hit the floor, Michael took the wallet from his hand. He had pulled the map partway out of the wallet when there was a knocking on the door.

"Tim, you in there? I thought I heard a gunshot. I called the cops and they're on the way. Tim?" the voice called again. Michael looked down at Tim lying on the floor and the gun in his own hand. Dropping Tim's wallet, which he held in his other hand, with the map still inside; he bolted out the back door to the alley that ran behind the house. He tucked the gun back into his jeans and made sure his shirt was covering it. Having his car parked down the street instead of in front of Tim's house worked out in his favor now. Making himself walk slowly to not attract attention, he circled back around and got into his car. As he was driving away, the sound of a siren caught his attention and when he looked in his rearview mirror, he saw the flashing lights of the police car as it pulled in front of Tim's house.

What the hell did you just do? he asked himself, tears

MARSHA DEFILIPPO

streaming down his face. Whatever had possessed him to kill his
friend was gone, and all that was left was fear and regret.

He had only driven a few blocks when it hit him he would
probably need an alibi. *Didn't the cops always ask friends and
relatives if they knew anything and where they were after
someone was murdered? That's what happened on TV and in the
movies.* He pulled over to park the car so he could think. After a
few minutes, he figured out what he should do. Pulling back onto
the street, he circled around to Tim's apartment. By the time he
got back, fire trucks, an ambulance, and cop cars were blocking
the street in front of the apartment. Pulling into a spot even
farther away than he'd been earlier, he parked the car and walked
up to the scene.

"What's going on?" he asked the cop who was making sure
no one went into the crime scene.

"There's been an incident. No one is allowed to go any closer," the cop told him.

Michael looked at the name tag on the officer's shirt.

"My friend lives in that apartment building, Officer Dube.
I'm supposed to meet him to hang out. That's why I'm here."

Officer Dube looked more closely at Michael, realizing he
wasn't just another looky-loo.

"What's your friend's name?"

"Timothy Nelson, but we all call him Tim. Can I at least go
tell him I'm here?"

"Wait here," Officer Dube told him before walking several
steps away and used his shoulder radio to speak with someone.
"I've got a guy here who says he's a friend of Timothy Nelson's.
They were planning to get together today."

Michael could hear the response but waited until Officer
Dube walked back to where he was waiting to repeat the
message.

"Someone will be right down. Just wait here."

Michael looked toward the cluster of first responders and

saw one break away to walk in their direction. Once there, he reached out his hand for Michael to shake.

"I'm Detective Smith. And you are?"

"My name's Michael Granger. But what's going on? I'm here to see my friend, Tim Nelson, who lives in that apartment building. Is he okay?" Michael hoped his expression looked like someone who was concerned, but unaware of what was happening.

"You know Timothy Nelson?"

"Yeah, we've been friends all our lives. We grew up together and our families have known each other even longer. You didn't answer my question. Is Tim okay?"

"What's your phone number and address, Mr. Granger?" the detective asked, pulling out a notebook and pen from his inside jacket pocket.

Michael played along and gave him the information.

"I've told you what you want. Now answer my question. Is Tim okay?"

"I'm sorry, Mr. Granger. I'm not at liberty to say, but Mr. Nelson was expecting you?"

Keep playing the part and act angry, the voice in his head told him.

"I'm done. Unless you can tell me about my friend, I'm not answering any more of your questions." Michael looked directly into the cop's eyes, making sure not to flinch or give away how nervous he was. He had no other alibi, so it was crucial to convince the cop he was clueless about what had happened.

"As I told you, Mr. Granger. I'm not at liberty to say. You might as well go home, but make sure you stay available if we have any other questions." With that, he turned and walked back to the crime scene.

"He's dead, isn't he? That's why you're not saying anything..." Michael called out and attempted to follow, but

Officer Dube blocked his path. Detective Smith continued walking, ignoring Michael's comments.

"You heard the man. There's no reason for you to be hanging around," he told him, but his tone was conciliatory.

Michael shrugged him off and gave Dube one last look before walking back to his car.

I think it worked, he told himself, hoping it was true.

CHAPTER TWENTY-THREE

~

*M*ichael made a point of watching the six o'clock news in case they reported Tim's death. He would have to talk to Bill about it, but couldn't until the news was public. Even if they didn't give out Tim's name, he could tell Bill it had to be him because of his encounter with the cops. He'd had the presence of mind to text Tim after he'd gotten back to his car to ask if he was okay and let him know the cops weren't letting him near the apartment. There would obviously be no answer, but it might give him more credibility if he kept up the pretense. If they checked Tim's phone records, Michael's number would be in the log, backing up his story that they had made plans to be together at Tim's apartment.

The news didn't disappoint.

The body of a man who had been fatally wounded was found by the police early this afternoon after a 911 call reporting a gunshot coming from the apartment where the victim lived. The police do not have any additional information to report at this time and the victim's name is being withheld pending notification of family. We will keep you updated as more information becomes available.

Michael took a couple of deep breaths to settle himself before calling Bill.

"Hey, Mikey, what's up?"

"I think Tim may be dead."

"*What?* That's not funny, man."

"I'm serious, Bill. Tim called this morning to invite me to come up to check out his new apartment and have some burgers. When I got close to his apartment, there were cops and fire trucks and an ambulance blocking off the street in front of his apartment building. I tried getting the cops to tell me what was going on, but they wouldn't say anything even when I told them I was a friend of his. I tried texting Tim when I left, but he hasn't answered. I had a bad feeling about it, so I just watched the news. They're saying someone was fatally shot, but they can't give out the name until they notify the family. It has to be him."

"Did you call his folks?"

"No. What if it wasn't him? I didn't want to get them all upset for nothing."

"That makes sense."

There was silence on the line, but Michael waited for Bill to continue.

"Who would want to kill Tim?"

"I don't have any idea. Maybe it was just random," Michael offered.

"Had to be," Bill agreed. "There's no other explanation."

"I'm sorry to lay this on you over the phone, but I didn't want you to find out from someone else. Maybe it's not him and there's some other reason he hasn't gotten back to me."

"Maybe. But I think you're right. If he hasn't texted or called you back, it has to be him."

"Call me when you're back in town. We should know more by then."

"I will and you do the same if you hear something sooner."

Promising to do that, Michael disconnected the call.

He let out his breath in relief. *Maybe you should consider an acting career. That was an Academy award performance, right there,* he told himself.

CHAPTER TWENTY-FOUR

～

"Annalise, have you heard the news?" Sarah's panicked voice came over the line.

"I haven't had a chance to read the paper yet. I had an early session booked this morning. What's wrong, Sarah? You sound upset."

"Timothy Nelson was murdered."

"Timothy Nelson? Who is he?" Annalise asked, not registering the connection.

"He's the great-grandson of John Nelson. The one Frank Abbott told us Harvey Granger killed to steal his piece of the map. This has to be more than a coincidence."

A chill ran down Annalise's spine.

"You're sure it's the same one?"

"Ninety-nine percent. The address didn't match what I had, but the news said he'd just recently moved to Bangor from Belfast, so that matches."

"Do the police have a suspect?"

"Not yet, unless they've found someone since the paper came

out, but there was no update on TV either. That means that whoever killed him is still on the loose. And if it has anything to do with the break-in at your house, you might be in danger."

"Thanks for letting me know, Sarah. I'll be extra careful, and I'll call the security company to ask if they can put a rush on installing the alarm system."

"Would you please check in with me through the day, so I'll know you're alright? Even if it's just a text with a thumb's up emoji, that would be good enough."

"I have a couple more Reiki sessions scheduled for today, but I'll try to remember to do that in between clients. I don't think anyone will try something if they see cars in the driveway."

"What about tonight?"

"I'll figure something out. My next appointment just pulled in. I'll talk to you later and thanks again for the warning, Sarah."

Annalise was good at compartmentalizing. It was a necessary part of the work she did when the focus had to be entirely upon her client during the session. Today, though, she was struggling to keep her thoughts from wandering to Sarah's phone call. She made herself a promise to meditate once she was done for the day to attempt to tune into any sense of impending danger. That put her mind at ease and she was able to make it through the rest of her appointments. After every session she made sure she sent Sarah a text letting her know she was okay.

It was late afternoon before she was done with her clients and had time for her meditation. Her preferred place for that was in her bedroom's sitting room. It wasn't a place where she *had* to be for her meditations, but setting the mood with music, candle-light, and incense had become a part of that ritual. Looking through her boxes of incense, she picked a stick from the one that contained Nag Champa, placed it in her incense burner and lit it. Next, she lit the candle that was already on the table next to her chair. She was still old-school and hadn't yet given up her CD player to replace it with streaming music. After selecting one from what she called her spa collection, she turned on the music and then sat in the chair beside the window facing the trees at the far end of her property. She took several deep breaths and relaxed her vision until the trees became a soft green blur, and her mind achieved a meditative state. She saw the face of the man she had seen in the diner. He had an expression of shock as he looked down at the still body of a man. Then Annalise saw what looked like a piece of yellowed paper sticking out of a wallet next to the body. Something caught the man's attention, and he looked up before turning and running out of the house and the image was gone. Annalise's focus returned to her room, and she sat for a moment replaying what she had seen in her mind. She did a quick body scan to determine if she felt any immediate danger and was relieved to find she did not. She felt a sense of something more to come, though, and she should be vigilant of her surroundings.

After sending a text to Sarah reassuring her that she was safe and that she wouldn't send any more messages unless that changed, she made her way downstairs to start cooking her dinner.

The sense of unease remained in her subconscious for the rest of the night, though, and her last thought before going to sleep was that she needed to call the alarm company in the morning.

CHAPTER TWENTY-FIVE

~

*W*hen the text notification pinged the next morning, Annalise picked up her phone to read the group text Sarah had sent to the Cozy Quilts Club group.

> I've got more information to share. We should get together ASAP.

BEFORE SHE HAD a chance to reply, another text came in from Eva.

> Can everyone meet at my house tonight at 7?

> I can come.

Annalise read Jennifer's reply and then added her own.

> Me, too. See you tonight!

An atmosphere of anticipation hung in the air when the group assembled at Eva's dining room table, stirring up a mix of excitement and dread.

"I've already talked to Annalise about this, but did you see the report about the murder in Bangor of Timothy Nelson?" Sarah asked Jennifer and Eva.

"I saw something on the news but didn't pay much attention," Jennifer said.

"Same here," Eva said.

"That's the first part of why I asked to meet tonight. You must not have connected the name, but he's the same Nelson who was the great-grandson of John Nelson; the one Frank Abbott told us was killed by Harvey Granger."

Both Jennifer and Eva gasped.

"Do you think that's connected to what's happening now with the discovery of his body and the news story about the treasure map?" Jennifer asked.

"It *might* be a coincidence, but I don't think so," Sarah said.

"It isn't," Annalise announced, and all eyes turned to her.

"I did a meditation last night. In the vision that came to me, I saw a man looking down at the body of another man and beside him was a wallet with a piece of paper sticking out of it. I'm sure it was one of the pieces of the map and the man who was looking at the body was the same one I saw at the diner."

There was silence as everyone digested that bit of news. Even Reuben was being quieter than usual. Sarah broke the somber mood by reaching into her backpack and pulling out a stack of papers, which she placed on the table. Shuffling through, she picked one out and placed it in front of Annalise. It was the mug shot of a man Annalise recognized as the one she'd seen, although he was younger when the photo was taken.

"That's him. He's related to Harvey Granger?" she asked Sarah when she saw the name Michael Granger on the mug shot.

"Yes, he's a great-grandson, too."

"This is history repeating itself," Annalise said quietly, more to herself than the others.

"What do we do about it, though?" Eva asked. "The original plan was to turn over the piece you have to Granger's descendant, since we assumed Harvey had the other two pieces. I think that would be too dangerous now, especially after he was willing to kill Timothy Nelson for it."

"We're in the same position as we were with Aunt Sadie. We can't go to the police based on your having a vision about Michael Granger," Jennifer said.

"And how I got some of this information isn't exactly kosher," Sarah said, "so there's no easy way to explain how you found the connections to them if they asked."

"The stakes are even higher now. At least before, it was just a matter of contacting Harvey's heirs and telling them they could have the other piece. Now that there's been a murder, we have an obligation to get the authorities involved somehow," Annalise said.

"We also don't know if William Robinson is involved," Sarah said. "He's Frank Abbott's descendant," she added to remind the others.

"Has the security company installed your alarm system?" Eva asked.

Annalise had been hoping to avoid that topic, but now it wasn't an option.

"I called them this morning to ask about the status and was told they were going to have to reschedule because they didn't have one of the parts they needed. It looks like it's going to be at least another two weeks because it's on back-order. But I'm not sensing any immediate danger for me. I'll be okay in the meantime," she continued when she saw the looks of concern on everyone's face.

"I may not be a psychic, but I'm pretty sure there's no way we can talk you into staying out of your house until the police catch Michael Granger. Assuming they figure out he's the one who killed Timothy Nelson," Eva said.

"You would be right," Annalise said with a smile. "I have clients scheduled and I'm not going to let Granger and maybe Robinson, too, scare me out of my own house. But if I have any hint I would be in danger, I promise I'll reconsider."

"In that case, there's not anything more we can do about this tonight. Unless you have something else in your research we should know about," Eva said to Sarah.

"Nothing that would change the current situation."

"We came up with a way to catch Stephen Hill. Maybe we can come up with a plan to catch Michael Granger," Jennifer said hopefully.

"It wouldn't hurt to try," Eva said, but no one showed any confidence they thought they would be successful or had any suggestions for what the plan would be.

CHAPTER TWENTY-SIX

*E*va had persuaded Annalise to join her for dinner the following evening, but hadn't told her she had also invited her partner, Jim Davis, until Annalise arrived. As a retired state police officer, he still had contacts in law enforcement and had been instrumental in helping the Cozy Quilts Club members meet with the detectives investigating the murder of Jennifer's aunt Sadie the previous month. In the course of telling Jim how they learned who her killer was, Eva had to reveal they had used their paranormal skills to trap the killer into making a confession. They had told a white lie to the detectives on the case about Eva learning the killer's identity by talking to Sadie's dog, who had been a witness to the murder. Because they had knowledge of details only someone at the scene would have known, it was true they had been able to convince the killer they were onto him. Nevertheless, they were fully aware that convincing the detectives was another matter. It had only been after proving to Jim that Eva could speak to animals through a demonstration with her cat, Reuben, that they felt confident enough to ask for his help. For their demonstration, Jim had thought of something he had never shared with anyone, and Reuben passed along the information to Eva. To make sure he wouldn't think it was a fluke, they'd done it one more time. It had made Jim a believer. Not that he would say so to any of his law enforcement buddies! There was more than enough bad press about using psychics to solve cases. Eva had hatched a plan that together with Annalise, they were going to tell Jim what they had learned about the treasure hunters, past and present, and ask for his advice about how they should proceed.

"Do you really think he'll be able to help?" Annalise asked once Eva revealed her idea.

"He might not come up with a plan tonight, but if he has all the information we do, he might later. If nothing else, we have one more person who knows what we do is real, and he knows how cops think so he'd have a lot better chance of coming up with something they'll believe. They still trust him, even after the confession Stephen Hill made when we told him Boscoe revealed it was him. I was on tenterhooks waiting to hear if they would follow up or just file the report in the wastebasket."

"Good point. We'll just have to try our best to come up with a plan they'll at least listen to and hope it's enough to head them in the right direction before Michael Granger tries to break in again."

Jim arrived with a bottle of wine, which Eva suggested they take to the screened porch and chat for a while before dinner. The air was warm but for a change; the humidity was low, and between the wine, the comfy chairs, and sounds of nature and the water fountain just outside the porch, everyone was relaxed. Reuben had come, too, and stretched himself out on the loveseat next to Eva. He took up all the space beside her, so Jim sat in the Adirondack chair facing Eva and Annalise was in the other to his right.

Eva and Annalise exchanged a glance, and Annalise gave a brief nod for Eva to begin.

"We have something we'd like to run by you," she began.

"And here I was thinking you'd invited me just for the pleasure of my company," he teased.

"That's a given," Annalise teased back.

"I've told you the story about Annalise's family being a part of the article in The Bangor News about the treasure hunters. And, of course, you know about the break-in at her house. More has happened since then, but I'll let Annalise pick it up from here."

"I asked Sarah to contact Frank Abbott. He's the man who came to my great-grandparent's house back in 1926 and died that night. I hoped he would tell us the last names of the other two men. She was able to speak with Frank and he told her who they were. The one whose body was just found was John Nelson and the one who killed him, and Frank Abbott, was named Harvey Granger. After learning their names and that they had all lived in Belfast then, she had enough information to do some research into genealogy records and newspaper articles. Harvey was able to get away with the murders because he told the authorities John and Frank were in the other boat they had taken for their camping trip and it had capsized. He claimed he tried to rescue them, but he couldn't make it in time because of the storm. The bodies were never found, which they wouldn't have been because they weren't there. People just assumed the current carried them out to sea. She found records to trace all of their descendants to the present day." She paused, considering how to proceed.

'After Sarah got that information, I met with her and Eva at The Checkout Diner for lunch and Sarah filled us in on who the current descendants are. When we were getting ready to leave the diner, a man who had been sitting at the counter went out ahead of us, but he looked at me just as he was going out the door and our eyes met. I instantly felt a sense of recognition and a vision came to me of him holding my jewelry box that the map is hidden in."

"That was the day you asked me to meet you and Eva at your house until your cousin came?" Jim asked.

"Oh, that's right. You already know that part. Later I did a meditation, and I saw the image of a man looking down at the body of another man lying on the floor and I could tell he was dead. There was a wallet on the floor beside him with a piece of paper sticking out of it, and I knew it was a piece of the treasure map. The face of the man who was standing there was the same one I'd seen in the diner."

"Do you think it's possible you imagined his face because you had just seen him in the diner?"

"That's a valid question, but no, I don't. Sarah suggested we all meet because she had more information she wanted to share with us. When I told everyone about my vision, she pulled out the mugshot of the same man. His name is Michael Granger and he's the great-grandson of Harvey Granger. I think he's also the person who killed Timothy Nelson."

"His murder was on the news a couple of days ago. Sarah's research traced him as the descendant of John Nelson. We're ninety-nine percent positive he is the one whose skeletal remains were found that started this whole adventure," Eva told Jim.

"But how do you tell this to the police, right?" Jim asked.

"That's exactly it. And where you come in," Eva grinned.

Jim groaned. "I was afraid you were going to say that."

"Your help solving Sadie Emerson's murder was invaluable. We wouldn't have been able to have the police take us seriously if you hadn't been with Jennifer. Now we need to find a way to let them know the identity of the body found under the boat is John Nelson and Michael Granger is the one who killed Timothy Nelson. So, any suggestions?" Annalise asked.

"Not off the top of my head, but let me sleep on it and see if some inspiration comes to me."

"I knew we could count on you," Eva said.

"Don't thank me yet. I may not think of anything."

"We'll be thinking, too. If we all put our heads together, one of us is bound to come up with something," Eva said.

CHAPTER TWENTY-SEVEN

"*I* think we need some retail therapy," Eva said after she had exchanged greetings with Annalise.

Annalise laughed. "You probably won't have to twist my arm. Anyplace special you'd like to go?"

"Quilting Essentials is always on the top of my list. I really do need some thread, but I'd like to browse the rest of the store, too."

"Sounds good. I can meet you there in half an hour. I'll have to be back by three-thirty to be ready for my four o'clock appointment, but that should be plenty of time. And might be a good thing, since I won't have as much time to find more things to buy."

Eva's car was already in the parking lot when Annalise arrived, and she found her inside checking out the thread selections. She waved to Evelyn Jackson, the shop's owner, who had greeted her from the back of the store when she walked in.

"Finding what you were looking for?" she asked Eva, who hadn't noticed her approaching.

"Not yet. I just got here a couple of minutes ago. What do you think? This one," she asked, holding up a shade of pink against the swatch of fabric she had brought with her, "or this one?" as she held up a darker shade of pink.

"Are you using it for piecing or quilting?"

"Quilting. I'm thinking of doing some thread painting on the flowers to make them stand out more."

"Thread painting?" Annalise asked.

"That's when you add details with free motion quilting either on the design in the fabric itself or you are doing your own on a solid section—I think that's called the negative space, but I might be confusing the term. For this, I'm planning to use this flower and I'll stitch a series of vertical lines around the stamen to give it more definition and texture."

"Oh, right! I must have been having a senior moment. I've seen that before but wasn't making the connection. To say I've been distracted would be an understatement. I'd go with the darker pink."

"I can't imagine why you'd be distracted," Eva replied wryly.

"Can I help you ladies with anything?" Paul Taylor asked. Paul was the shop's machine technician who set up and repaired sewing machines for customers. He was also a quilter and his wife, Nicki, was the longarm quilter for the shop for those customers who preferred to hire someone else for that task.

"What do you think, light pink or dark pink to do thread painting on this section?" Eva asked, pointing to the flower design.

"Dark pink."

"The choice is unanimous. Dark pink it is."

"The last time I saw you two was right after Sadie Emerson's murder. I read in the paper about your connection to the body found underneath the boat in the Kenduskeag. That was quite a story about the treasure map. I heard your quilting club helped solve Sadie's murder and her neighbor, Howard Smith's, too. You sure do lead interesting lives," he said.

"Sometimes too interesting," Annalise said, but didn't offer any further explanation.

"Like I told you then, you should come to one of our meetings. You never know what you'll be getting into besides quilting," Eva said, smiling. "In fact, why don't you come to our next one on Tuesday? We have a potluck supper first, but if you'd rather skip that, we start our projects around seven and wrap up between eight and eight-thirty. Do you have a project you're working on now?"

"That sounds like fun, and it might motivate me to make more progress on my project. A lot of times once we get home, Nicki and I just eat our dinner and watch TV the rest of the evening."

"We'd love to have you. It would be nice to have another person's ideas and to have you share your expertise would be wonderful, especially with free-motion quilting." Annalise said.

"You've convinced me. If I remember correctly, you told me the meetings are held at your house?" he asked Eva.

"That's right. I can give you my address now to make sure you have it."

Paul pulled out his phone and added Eva's contact information.

"I'll let you know if something comes up, but otherwise, I'll see you both next Tuesday at seven," he said and left to assist another customer.

"Oh, look at these kits to make fabric baskets!" Annalise said, walking over to the display.

"So pretty! And it has everything you need to make it except, wait for it… thread," Eva said, and they both laughed as they walked back to the thread display to select a color for Annalise's project.

CHAPTER TWENTY-EIGHT

ho can that be? Annalise asked herself when her doorbell chimed. She didn't have any clients scheduled until later in the afternoon. She looked out the side-light before opening the door and saw two men in suits standing on her porch giving off the vibe they were there on official business. Not getting a warning anything was amiss, she opened the door.

"Good morning. Can I help you?"

They each held up an ID as the taller one introduced them.

"My name is Detective Roberts, and this is my partner, Detective Smith. May we come in to ask you a few questions?"

Annalise remembered their names from Sadie Emerson and Howard Smith's murder investigations. Jim hadn't mentioned contacting them after their discussion at Eva's, so at first she was surprised about their arrival, but her instinct told her this had to be related to the treasure map.

"Of course. We can talk in here," she said, leading them into the living room and gesturing for them to take a seat in the chairs as she walked to the couch facing them. "Can I offer you some-thing to drink? I have a fresh pot of coffee, or perhaps a drink of water?"

"Thank you for the offer, but we're fine," Detective Roberts spoke for both of them. "We understand you have a piece of a treasure map that has been in your family since 1926."

"That's right. Susan Reynolds wrote a story about it for The Bangor News."

"Yes, ma'am, that's how we got that information," Detective Roberts continued. "We have reason to believe we may have another piece of that map and wondered if you would mind showing us yours to see if it is a match."

Annalise knew it did, but feigned ignorance.

"I don't mind at all, but can you tell me why you are asking about it now?"

The detectives exchanged a look before Roberts replied.

"We're not able to tell you how we got the map. It's part of an ongoing investigation," Detective Smith said.

"I see. If this is important to a crime you're investigating, I'm happy to help. I'll need to go upstairs to get it, but I'll only be a moment."

On the way to retrieve the map from her jewelry box, Annalise debated whether she should bring up the break-in at her house. She had no way to prove it was connected or that Michael Granger had not only been the one who orchestrated the break-in, but was also the same person who killed Timothy Nelson in what she believed was a dispute over the map. She remembered Sarah saying some of her methods hadn't been entirely above-board when she did her research, and she didn't want to get her in trou-ble. That would be a problem if the detectives asked questions she wouldn't be able to answer without telling them *how* she got information about the current descendants of Harvey Granger. She could play innocent, though, and gloss over that she already knew who it was who had broken in. Perhaps it would be worthwhile to put the thought in their heads the two events were connected, even if she couldn't give them Michael Granger's name.

"Here it is," she said, holding out the piece to Detective Roberts, who took the other piece out of his jacket pocket. It was in an evidence bag but was unfolded so he could lay her piece over it to see if it matched.

"It's a match," he said after turning Annalise's piece to the right orientation to align with the piece he brought.

"Do you think it's connected to the break-in at my house?"

Both detectives looked at her with a puzzled expression.

"Your house was broken into, and you think there's a connection?"

"Yes. It happened shortly after the story appeared in The Bangor News. Nothing was taken but from the way the house was disturbed, it looked like the burglar was looking for something specific. Deputy Tremblay... his first name is Carl, if I remember correctly... came to the scene and took my statement. There should be a report on file."

Detective Smith wrote the information down in the notebook he had taken from his coat pocket.

"We'll be sure to talk to Deputy Tremblay. I assume you haven't had any follow up from the police about this?"

"No, but I wasn't expecting to. Now that you showed up, though, it made me wonder if there was more than you've told me."

"This is the first we've heard of the break-in at your house," Detective Roberts said. "Getting back to the map, though, is there any additional information you can tell us beyond what was in the newspaper article?"

I could, but you wouldn't believe me, she thought. Aloud, she said, "Not at the moment, but if I think of something later, I'll be sure to let you know."

They each handed her their business cards, thanked her for her time, and left.

I need to get in touch with Jim. He's going to have to be involved so I can make my case to them about Michael Granger and have them believe me. She didn't have his number, but she would call Eva to coordinate a meeting.

CHAPTER TWENTY-NINE

~

*E*va and Jim arrived at her house the next day, and they gathered at the kitchen table with coffee and cinnamon buns Annalise had baked that morning.

"Thanks for coming. I realize I'm asking a lot of you, but you know the detectives who came to my house yesterday and have already worked with them on Sadie's murder. What impression did you have about their reaction when Jennifer played the recording of us telling Stephen Hill that Boscoe had told Eva he was the killer?"

Jim chuckled at the memory of when the conversation they had recorded was played for the detectives and it got to that part.

"It's a good thing we prepared them you'd told a white lie to convince Hill you knew facts about what happened which no one should know because there were no witnesses. Or at least, no witnesses he thought could implicate him. Otherwise, any credibility Jennifer had might have gone out the window. I was just happy they didn't press it to ask exactly how you knew what you did. I didn't have any Plan B."

"Hmmm. There must have been a part of them that had to buy into the story to keep investigating so what's your opinion of whether they'd give me the benefit of the doubt if I told them Michael Granger is the one who broke into my house and most likely killed Timothy Nelson?"

Jim considered the question before answering.

"Honestly, I think it was because they'd hit a dead end. And they had the DNA they sent to the lab to see if it matched the drops of blood found near Sadie's body."

Both Annalise's and Eva's shoulders slumped in defeat at hearing this.

"You're probably right. We don't have any way of getting Michael Granger to make a confession like we did with Stephen Hill. Unless the detectives can tie him into the scene with actual evidence, he could possibly get away with this," Eva said.

"And in the meantime, you're still in danger if Michael decides to come back," Jim said to Annalise.

CHAPTER THIRTY

~

*P*aul Taylor was the last to arrive at the next meeting and even though Eva and Annalise told him it wasn't necessary to bring anything, he had a covered dish and a small paper bag in one hand and his rolling sewing machine case in the other when Eva opened the door.

"Welcome, Paul! Everyone else is in the kitchen. Let me take that for you," she said, reaching for the covered dish, "and I'll show you where you can set up your machine."

"I hope it's alright that I'm early. I know you said it was okay to come after the potluck dinner, and it wasn't necessary to bring anything. When I told Nicki, she insisted I couldn't come empty-handed, so she made a spinach artichoke dip and added a box of crackers for dipping. And here I am," he said sheepishly.

"No need to apologize and it's no problem at all you're here early. That's my favorite dip! Please thank Nicki for us. We always have plenty to eat so you won't be taking anyone's share of the dinner."

"Paul brought spinach artichoke dip and crackers," Eva

announced when they reached the kitchen to the cheers of every-one. "Sharon, have you met Paul? He's the machine technician at Quilting Essentials. His wife, Nicki, taught the free motion quilting class that first brought us all together and he filled in for one of the classes."

"I'm pleased to meet you," Paul said, holding out his hand for Sharon to shake.

"Pleased to meet you, too. It's good to have another newbie to the Club."

"I'll show Paul where to set up and be right back. Why don't you all start with the appetizers while you're waiting?"

They returned a couple minutes later to find the women gath-ered in the dining room enjoying the dip and the charcuterie tray Jennifer brought and after getting themselves a drink, went in to join them.

"We were just trying to talk Annalise into staying with Sharon, but she's not cooperating," Jennifer said, but her tone was lighthearted.

"I've already told you I'm not going to be chased out of my house and the alarm system should be installed soon."

"Has the security company given you an update about when the parts will be in?" Eva asked.

Sarah noticed Paul's expression of confusion and jumped in to explain.

"You might not have heard about Annalise's house being broken into. We think it's connected to the piece of the treasure map she has, and the remains found under the boat in the Kenduskeag River. Did you know about that?"

"I saw the article in The Bangor News about the map and the story she'd been told about how her grandfather got it, but I didn't know about the break-in."

"It happened shortly after that article came out and it looked like whoever broke in was trying to find something specific because of the way they'd gone through my house, but nothing was taken. It seemed like too much of a coincidence," Annalise explained.

"We've been worried they would come back to try again since they didn't find the map the first time," Sarah said. "Annalise has made arrangements to have an alarm system installed, but it's taking longer than expected. In the meantime, she could be in danger if she is at home if or when they do come back."

"Have you thought about just offering to give your piece of the map to the person who has the other ones? I'm guessing you didn't have any plans to try looking for it yourself."

"No, I think my treasure hunting days are long over, even if I had all the pieces," Annalise said, smiling. "I have thought about giving it back. It would be the perfect solution."

"But how would you get it to them? Would you really want to meet with them after what they've done?" Sarah asked.

Annalise shook her head imperceptibly to stop Sarah from saying any more to give away they already knew who had the other pieces and that Michael Granger had killed Timothy Nelson over the map. The others noticed and kept quiet as well.

"What if you talked to the reporter again? Have her do a story to say you want to give it to whoever has the other pieces? It would probably be better than a classified ad," Paul suggested.

Annalise nodded. "I'm going to think about it some more, but that's actually not a bad idea. Now that we've got that figured out, let's finish eating so we can begin the best part of the evening, which is our sewing projects. Speaking of which, didn't you say something about wanting to have Nicki quilt one of your tops, Jen?"

As she'd hoped, that redirected the conversation. Annalise's thoughts were spinning. Paul's suggestion really was a good one and just might be the way to lure Michael Granger into a trap. She just needed to work out some more details.

Jennifer realized what Annalise was doing and followed her lead.

"You're right, I do. Do you know what Nicki's schedule is like? I'm not in a rush, but would like to take it off my UFO pile. That's an unfinished object in quilt-speak," she said to Sharon when she saw the puzzled look on her face.

Sharon chuckled and nodded her head. "I get it now."

"I don't think she's backed up at the moment, but you should bring it in sooner than later, before the orders start coming in for holiday gifts."

"I can bring it in tomorrow if you think she'll be available."

"She will be working all day, so come whenever it's convenient for you."

"Thanks! I will."

～

"OKAY, everyone, it's time to call it a night for the sewing portion of our entertainment. It's time now to decide on next week's theme and draw names. Do you think you'd like to come again next week?" she asked Paul and Sharon.

"This was fun. I'm in," Paul said.

"Me, too!"

After some discussion, they chose picnic food as their theme. Realizing that having two more people upset the distribution of the courses, they had a brief discussion before they agreed to add two side dishes to fit with the picnic menu. That settled, they each pulled a slip from the basket.

As everyone was packing up to leave, Eva found a way to speak to Annalise privately.

"I could practically see the wheels spinning in your head and it wasn't about quilting. What are you thinking?"

"Can't say now, but would you ask Jim to meet with us

tomorrow? I have an idea and want to pass it by him. It probably... no, definitely... is going to need his help."

"Of course. I'll text you when I find out what time works for him."

"Thanks, Eva," Annalise gave her a grateful smile. "I think it could work."

Annalise had finished the lock check and was about to head upstairs to bed when her text notification pinged.

> Jim can meet us tomorrow at eleven at my house.

> Perfect! Thanks for asking him and I'll see you both tomorrow.

CHAPTER THIRTY-ONE

~

*J*ennifer arrived the next day at Quilting Essentials with the quilt top she had spoken about with Paul. Evelyn Jackson greeted her as soon as she walked through the door.

"Jennifer, it's so good to see you. I don't think I've seen you since you took the free motion quilting class unless you came in at a time when I wasn't here."

"This is my first time back. Things got a little crazy after Aunt Sadie died. Has anyone told you about our quilting club that Eva, Annalise, Sarah, and I formed after the class? We're calling it the Cozy Quilts Club and we meet once a week. Last month we did crumb quilt projects, so I finally used up some of those small scraps I've been saving because I was convinced *someday* I would use them. And I have!"

"Paul told me about the club. Eva and Annalise told him about it when they were in last week. He mentioned they invited him to attend one of your meetings."

"Yes, in fact, he came to the one we had last night. You

should come to one sometime, too, if you can."

"Thank you. I may do that. To be honest, though, by the time I close up the shop, I've reached my daily quota of all things quilting, so don't be offended if I don't. It's nothing personal."

"I totally understand that."

"What can I help you with today?" Evelyn asked.

"I wanted to speak with Nicki about having one of my quilt tops finished. Paul said she would be here today and to come in anytime."

"Of course," Evelyn said. "I'll go tell her you're here."

Jennifer went to the section of the shop where the 108-inch-wide bolts were displayed to pick one out to use for the backing that would go with her quilt top. There was a large assortment of solids and prints in a variety of colors. When her mother had been quilting, she hadn't had as many options to choose from. Most quilters from that era pieced sections of material together to make a backing big enough for the size of the quilt they were making. Jennifer had considered making a backing from leftover fabric to create a secondary design for the quilt. That method had become popular in recent years. *Or was it an old method that had come back into fashion?* Jennifer wondered, considering how thrifty quilters had to be. They had been re-purposers long before it was a "thing". She had narrowed down her choices when she was joined by Nicki Taylor.

"Hi, Jennifer. Paul told me he had a great time at your quilt club meeting last night. Thank you for inviting him. He had fun, and I had a night for some me time without feeling guilty."

Jennifer laughed. "I know what you mean about that. Thinking about David and me being empty nesters in just a few years has me both excited about more me time, and sad the kids won't be around all the time. Thank you, too, for sending the dip and crackers. They were a hit with everyone. It was nice to have a guy's perspective as well. We're hoping he'll be able to join us more often."

"You won't have any objections from me. I love him dearly, but it would be good for both of us. He told me you might be coming in with a quilt top for me to quilt. It looks like you're picking out the backing," Nicki said, looking at the bolts Jennifer had removed from the shelf.

"Yes, I have it narrowed down to these two," Jennifer said, pointing to the two bolts of fabric in her shopping cart. "The solid matches one of the colors on the front and the paisley tone on tone has more contrast but still complements the colors in the design. What do you think?" Jennifer asked, holding up her quilt top which was still folded so only a portion of it was visible.

"Why don't we take them over to one of the classroom tables where we can spread them out next to your top so I can see how they look when I can see the whole design."

They spent the next half hour discussing the backing choices as well as what to use for the batting that would go between the top and back of the quilt, and Nicki made suggestions for designs she could use to quilt them all together.

"I think with the design you've done for the quilt top, an all-over quilting design makes sense. I could do custom quilting to add more design features, but that would significantly raise the cost because of the extra time it takes."

"An all-over design works. If I thought this might become an heirloom quilt, a custom design might be worth the extra money but for this, I'd rather keep the cost down."

They went to the cutting table after Jennifer had decided which backing she wanted to use and was about to head to the checkout area when Nicki stopped her.

"You know, you've got the skills to do this on your home machine after taking the free motion class, but the size does make it more challenging. Have you ever considered renting our longarm quilter?"

"I didn't know that was an option," Jennifer said, surprised.

"Not that I'm trying to talk you out of paying for my

services," Nicki said, smiling, "but, yes. We limit the class size to two people, so participants can have more hands-on instruction and it ends up being almost a private lesson. It's four hours long and costs one hundred dollars, but we then give you a credit of four hours to use for a future project, so it's like getting one free rental."

"I had no idea you did that," Jennifer said, her excitement evident. "I still want you to do the quilting for this one, but I want to at least give this a try. Maybe one of the other Cozy Quilters would be interested, too. Or maybe all of them!" she said, realizing they might all want to learn how to use the longarm machine. "I'll bring it up at next week's meeting and ask what they think and then come back to set up a class time even if it's only me."

"We do like to have two people in a class, so if you're the only one signing up, it might be a while before we get someone else. Would you be okay with taking a class with a stranger?"

"Absolutely! But I don't think that will be an issue."

They completed Jennifer's order just as Paul finished assisting another customer.

"You've been holding out on us, Paul," Jennifer said, faking displeasure.

"What did I do now, or maybe what didn't I do, considering your comment?" he asked, playing along.

"Nicki just told me about being able to rent time to use your longarm quilter and the class to learn how. If you still plan to come to next week's meeting, why don't you fill the rest of us in?"

"I'll be sure to do that. I probably won't be able to come every week. I don't want Nicki to feel ignored."

"Somehow, I suspect that won't be a problem," Jennifer said, giving Nicki a wink, and walked to the front of the store to pay for her purchases.

CHAPTER THIRTY-TWO

~

*A*nnalise was excited but nervous about Jim's reaction to the plan she had devised. It would mean meeting with Detectives Roberts and Smith and once again, giving them information about a killer that would require an explanation they might find hard to believe. She understood it was asking Jim to put *his* credibility on the line along with hers and she wouldn't blame him if he was reluctant to do that. She had to try, though.

Eva greeted her at the door even before she had a chance to ring the doorbell.

"Let me guess; Reuben told you I was here," Annalise said, looking over to where Reuben was sitting in the bay window. He jumped down and trotted over to her, rubbing his head against her leg. She bent down and obligingly scratched the top of his head and under his chin and was rewarded with an appreciative purr of thanks.

"You guessed right. Looks like he's in a good mood today," Eva noted, looking down at her cat.

I'm always in a good mood he retorted.

"Careful there, Pinocchio. You don't want your nose to start growing."

With that, he turned and walked back to his cushion and sat with his back facing them.

Annalise was able to fill in the blanks without Eva needing to explain.

"Jim's waiting in the screen room. I brought out a pitcher of lemonade and the leftovers from the dip and charcuterie to snack on while we chat."

Jim gave Annalise a smile, but he had a wary look in his eyes.

"Thanks for listening to my idea, Jim. I hope we'll still be friends after you've heard it."

"Now that doesn't make me worry at all. Or maybe I should say worry more."

"I guess we'll find out," Annalise said with a smile. "At last night's meeting, we were talking about the treasure map and how we think the break-in at my house is related. Paul suggested…"

"Who's Paul?" Jim interrupted.

"Paul Taylor. He and his wife, Nicki, work at Quilting Essentials. He's a quilter, too, so the last time Annalise and I saw him there, we invited him to come to a meeting, and last night was his first one," Eva explained.

"Okay, just trying to get context," Jim said.

"Paul suggested I give my piece of the map back to whoever has the other two pieces. I had thought about doing that before, but then it slipped my mind. He suggested I have Susan Reynolds do another story for The Bangor News to say I don't have any interest in the map and would like to give it back. As Paul said, it's probably better than putting an ad in the classifieds. It got me thinking maybe we could use it as a sting. We could put in the paper that the person interested should contact The Bangor News and they would coordinate the meeting to pass along my piece. There should probably be something about having to prove they really have the other pieces, and we would match them to mine to make sure they fit. I think even a photocopy would work if they're reluctant to bring the originals. "

"Sounds like a good plan. It isn't doing you any good, and worse, it's putting you in harm's way to keep it."

Annalise hesitated, searching for the best way to reveal the other part of the plan she hadn't wanted to discuss in front of Paul.

"It reminded me about how well it worked with Stephen Hill when we told him details about Sadie's murder we shouldn't have known. My idea is to have my phone on voice memos when we have the meeting to hand over the map and do the same with Michael Granger. I think I could make him confess to the break-in but more importantly, to the murder of Timothy Nelson."

"That's not a good idea. There were four of you when you met Stephen Hill. Even if you had the reporter with you, you could both be risking your safety and maybe your lives." Jim was adamant, but Annalise continued.

"What if I was wearing a wire instead? The police could be nearby for my protection, and they could record the conversation. And, hopefully, his confession."

"Now I see why I'm here," Jim said with resignation. "Walked right into that, didn't I?"

Annalise smiled.

"Did you know about this?" he asked Eva.

"The only thing I knew was that Annalise wanted to talk to you. She didn't want to take a chance of being overheard last night, so told me she'd explain today."

Jim sighed. "Is there more?" he asked Annalise.

"That about does it," Annalise said. "Well, maybe one thing. How do we convince the detectives they should agree to the sting and put a wire on me?"

"*One* more thing, Columbo?" he teased, and Annalise and Eva smiled, but said nothing.

"How do you think you can convince them it would be worth their time to do this since you don't have anything except circumstantial... well, it's not even evidence, circumstantial or otherwise," he realized, "information it's Michael Granger. I haven't heard anything about them even having a person of interest yet."

"Well, I'd have you with me to vouch for my character and that I'm not crazy or delusional. Did I remember to tell you they came to my house and wanted to see my piece of the map? They had read about it in the paper and had the piece I had seen in my vision. I asked them if they thought it was connected to the break-in at my house. They hadn't known about that, but it put the thought in their minds it could have been. I'm still working on the rest of how to phrase it all, but if it comes down to it, I would be okay with telling them I saw him in a vision. We might have to reveal Sarah's genealogy search, but I think we could do it in a way that wouldn't get her in trouble. A lot of that information is available for anyone to find. I suppose I could claim my grandfather actually had the other names, but I hadn't wanted to mention that to Susan Reynolds."

Jim still looked unconvinced, and Annalise was beginning to think it had been a waste of time.

"I guess it helps they've already met you and don't think you're crazy. Just for argument's sake, you would tell them you saw a vision of Michael Granger killing Timothy Nelson?"

"I didn't actually see him killing him. In my meditation, he was standing over the body and looking down at the wallet and the piece of the map that was sticking out. I suspect that bit of information is a holdback. It would have the same effect for them of asking themselves how I could know about it unless I really did have a vision about it."

Jim considered that. "I guess it's worth a try. The worst that happens is they laugh us out of the station, and I become the butt of jokes about the ex-cop who believes in psychics."

"No," Annalise said, "the worst that happens is they don't find out it's Michael Granger and put him away for murder."

Jim couldn't argue with that.

CHAPTER THIRTY-THREE

~

*S*arah emailed the mugshot to Annalise so she could print a copy to take with her. Jim had somehow been successful in setting up a meeting for them with Detectives Roberts and Smith, and he was picking her up in a few minutes. She heard Jim's car pull into her driveway and first taking a deep breath to calm her nerves, she locked the door behind her and walked out to meet him.

"Do you think it will work?" she asked once they were on their way.

"I give it a fifty-fifty chance. Maybe a little more. You helped them solve what they were afraid was going to turn into a cold case. Knowing you were a part of that gives you an edge."

Annalise nodded, and they both fell silent again. She closed her eyes and breathed deeply to center herself before beginning a silent Reiki session for herself and Jim, drawing in all the positive energy she could and hoped it would be enough. By the time they reached the station where they were meeting the detectives, she felt calm and confident they would be successful.

Jim gave their names to the officer on duty at the reception area and told them they had an appointment. Once that was confirmed, the officer handed each of them a visitor badge and instructed them to wait while he let the detectives know they were there.

Detective Smith was the one who came to bring them back to an interview room.

"Ms. Jordan. It's good to see you again. You, too, Jim. Follow me."

"I didn't realize this when we came to your house, but Jim told us you were one of the women who was there when Stephen Hill made his confession you all recorded. That was quite the story you ladies came up with, but it worked. We owe you all a thank you," Roberts began when they were gathered in the room.

"You're welcome. I hope that will give me some brownie points for what I'm about to propose to you. When you were at my house, I asked if the map could be connected to the break-in I'd had."

They both nodded their heads in acknowledgement they remembered.

"We need a way to draw out the person who did that. I have good reason to believe it was the same person who has the other pieces. My suggestion is that I ask Susan Reynolds to run another story saying I am willing to give my piece of the map to the person who has the other ones. I'm sure she would be able to phrase it in a way to entice them to come forward. We would have them contact The Bangor News to act as the intermediary to set up a meeting to do the exchange and you could fit me with a wire to catch his confession."

"Ms. Jordan, we're homicide detectives, not burglary. I am skeptical they'd be willing to do this for a break-in, especially since my understanding is nothing was taken," Roberts said, and Annalise could tell they were ready to dismiss her.

"I agree. But what if I told you I also believe the person who broke into my house is the same person who killed Timothy Nelson?"

As Roberts and Smith exchanged doubtful glances with each other as to whether this was worth more discussion, Annalise took the mugshot of Michael Granger out of her purse and put it on the table facing them.

"This is who you should be looking for."

CHAPTER THIRTY-FOUR

~

*T*he detectives had been examining the mugshot but looked up, their surprise evident at Annalise's proclamation.

"His name is Michael Granger, and he is a direct descendant of Harvey Granger. Harvey is the person who back in 1926 killed his partners Frank Abbott and John Nelson. Frank was the man who was helped by my great-grandparents, and John Nelson is the one whose skeletal remains were just found in the Kenduskeag River."

Annalise held her breath, hoping they wouldn't ask for more information about how she knew this, but luck was with her.

Detective Roberts still looked skeptical, but Dennis Smith picked up the mugshot for a closer look and then pulled his notebook from his coat pocket and flipped back a couple of pages.

"It is him," he said once he'd found the page he was looking for. "I saw this guy at the crime scene. He said his name was Michael Granger, and he was there to visit his friend, Tim Nelson. I didn't have any reason to suspect he wasn't telling the truth, so I took his contact information and told him we'd be in touch if we needed anything more."

That got Roberts's attention. *Maybe this would be easier than she'd expected,* she thought, and gave Jim an encouraging look. His interest had been piqued as well when Dennis Smith had made the connection between Timothy Nelson and Michael Granger.

"I'm more interested in having him arrested for Timothy Granger's murder than I am about the break-in. I would tell him I know he's a descendant of Harvey Granger and Timothy was a descendant of John Nelson and that, just like his grandfather, he was willing to commit murder to keep the map for himself. Then I would tell him I saw him standing over Timothy's body and there was a piece of the map sticking out of a wallet next to it. I think just like Stephen Hill, he would be so surprised I know that, he would admit it without realizing it was what he was doing."

The detectives were stunned. That detail about the murder had been a holdback, just as Annalise had suspected. No one outside of the police department should have knowledge about it.

"How do you know about the wallet and the piece of the map?" Dennis Smith finally asked. "That hasn't been released."

"I would be telling the truth. I did see him standing over Timothy Nelson's body and the wallet with the piece of the map beside it. This probably isn't something you want to believe, but I sometimes receive information through visions."

"You mean you're a psychic?" Roberts asked.

"I don't make a habit of telling that to most people, but yes."

"Did you know about this?" Roberts asked Jim, a hint of anger in his voice.

Jim shifted in his chair, but looked both Roberts and Smith directly in the eye before answering. "I did, and I believe her. I didn't realize she was going to mention it, though," he said, looking at Annalise and she saw the expression of betrayal on his face.

"I'm sorry, Jim. I didn't plan to tell them, but I couldn't think of any other way to explain how I would convince Michael to confess to the murder. I would have to tell him I knew he was there, or he wouldn't confess. That's kind of the whole point of this."

There was another long silence, and Annalise's earlier confidence about convincing the detectives to go along with her sting idea was fading. Her intuition was nudging her to push the idea anyway.

"So, what do you think? Should I get in touch with Susan Reynolds to run the story?" Annalise asked to break the silence.

Dennis Smith shrugged as he looked at Phil Roberts. "It's a crazy idea, but it might work just like she said happened with Stephen Hill. I don't think we should use *the psychic said he did it* approach to ask the boss, but maybe we can come up with another way."

Phil Roberts didn't look convinced, but nodded his agreement.

"We would need to have approval for this first from higher up in the chain of command," Smith said. "If you would hold off on speaking to Susan Reynolds for now, we'll be in touch one way or the other."

"Of course." Annalise told them, but she had already decided with or without their help, she was going to do this. If not with a wire, she could still record Michael Granger's confession. She had no doubt he was guilty, and she would find the way to make him admit it.

CHAPTER THIRTY-FIVE

~

*F*our days later, she finally got a call from Detective Roberts.

"It wasn't easy, but we finally got the thumbs up to go ahead with your idea."

"That's wonderful! What happens now?"

"You reach out to Susan Reynolds and convince her to run the story about handing over your map piece. You should tell her you think he might have been involved with the break in because of his connection to the map. For that reason, you want the exchange to happen in a public place, like a coffee shop or restaurant, so he won't get any ideas about trying something with witnesses around. If he was involved with the break-in at your house, you wouldn't want to be taking any chances. That's why I would be with you, pretending to be a friend of yours. He hasn't seen me, so I will join you, pretending to be from The Bangor News."

"Wouldn't that make Michael suspicious? If Susan Reynolds is the one reporting the story, why would a man be coming?"

"I'll say something came up at the last minute to keep her from coming and she asked me to come in her place."

"Of course, that makes perfect sense. How would I explain to *her* why you would be there instead of her?"

"You can say you thought he would be less likely to try anything if you have a man with you instead of a woman. You should not, under any circumstances, tell her about our involvement as part of the murder of Timothy Nelson. We don't want to take any chances Michael Granger would find out you believe he killed him."

"What if she insists on coming, too?"

Roberts was quiet for a moment while Annalise waited, knowing he was going over scenarios in his mind.

"I'd rather not have her there in case anything makes him suspicious. Tell her you're afraid he might not want to say anything about the break-in if there are too many people and emphasize you feel it's better to have a man instead of a woman for safety's sake. I realize that's sexist, but whatever it takes."

"I'll do my best to convince her she shouldn't come. As soon as I hear from her about whether she'll do the article, I'll let you know."

CHAPTER THIRTY-SIX

*a*s soon as she had disconnected the call with Roberts, she phoned Susan Reynolds who answered on the first ring. Even though she had been hoping for days to receive the go-ahead to set it up, she still felt butterflies in her stomach.

"Hello, this is Susan Reynolds."

"Susan, it's Annalise Jordan."

"Hi! Do you have another great story about treasure hunters?"

"Not exactly, but it is related. I don't know if you're aware I had a break-in at my house shortly after the story was printed?"

"Oh, no! I didn't know that. Are you alright? Were you home when it happened?"

"Fortunately, I wasn't at home at the time, but when I got home, it was obvious that whoever had broken in was looking for something specific. Nothing was stolen, including my piece of the map. I've been on edge ever since, though, and have decided I want to give it back. I haven't felt safe ever since it happened, but if the map is gone, there would be no reason to attempt it a second time. That's where you come in."

"You want me to do a follow-up story to put the word out?" Susan asked.

"Exactly! No putting one over on you," Annalise chuckled.

"My momma didn't raise no fools," Susan replied, using the time-honored retort. "What would you like me to say in the article?"

"Don't say anything about the break-in, of course. I wouldn't want to scare them off if it is the same person. Just say I realize there must be someone out there who has had the map pieces all these years and I would like to give mine to them. I have no interest in trying to find the treasure but if they want to, they're welcome to it. I'd also like to have you be the contact person to arrange the meeting if you're willing to do that. It wouldn't be necessary for you to come with me, as I have someone I trust who I can bring, so I wouldn't be going alone."

After having had the time to think about the discussion she'd had with the detectives at the station, she realized keeping it simple would be the best way to not have Susan asking more questions. She was too sharp to try to deceive her with their ulterior motives. If she stuck to the story of giving the piece back so she wouldn't have to worry about more attempts to break into her house, it would be more convincing. She held her breath now, hoping it had worked.

"Do you have a meeting place in mind? Susan asked.

"I was thinking The Daily Drip coffee shop on Central Street would be a suitable location. It's easy enough to find and even though my friend is a man, being in a public spot would make me feel safer. That wouldn't be in the actual article, of course. I leave it up to you to print the specifics of how they should get in touch to arrange the day and time."

"How would you know it's the right person and not someone just pretending to have the other pieces?"

"That didn't occur to me at first, but then I realized having just the one piece of the map wouldn't do anyone any good. It might make your life easier to cut down on calls from imposters who don't think about that, if you say I want to see the other pieces to make sure mine completes the map."

"That makes sense," Susan agreed. "Sure, I can write the story for you. It wouldn't be front page news, but I'm sure my editor would agree to do it as a follow-up. There hasn't been any update on the identity of the remains they found, but that isn't surprising considering how long they had been there."

Annalise hoped Susan would forgive her for not revealing she did know who it was, both regarding the body which had been found or who she expected to show up for the piece she had. After Michael had been arrested and was no longer a threat, she would call Susan again to clue her in. If this kept up, she was going to have to add her number to her Favorites list on her phone. Instead, she thanked Susan for agreeing to write this part of the story and disconnected the call.

CHAPTER THIRTY-SEVEN

~

Sharon and Paul had joined them for the next Cozy Quilts Club meeting, and everyone was in a festive mood. It had been a beautiful summer day, one of those rare ones that was just the right combination of warmth and humidity. They had gathered in Eva's screen room to chat while they ate the appetizers. In keeping with the picnic theme they had picked at their last meeting, Eva had spread a red and white gingham check tablecloth on the coffee table which they were sitting around. The fragrance of flowers from her garden was in the air and the sounds of birds chirping in the trees and at the feeder and insects buzzing was a perfect backdrop.

"I have some news to share with you," Annalise announced. "Susan Reynolds is doing another follow-up story about the treasure map. After Paul made the suggestion at the last meeting, I asked her to print a story offering my piece of the map to whoever has the other pieces. I told her about the break-in and since I had no plans to go after the treasure even if I had the other pieces, it might make me feel safer with it not in the house."

"That was a great idea, yours and yours," Jennifer said first to Paul and then Annalise.

"She's not going to put the part about the break-in in the article because obviously it would spook them off if they are the one who did it. But I figured if I told her that part of the story off the record, she'd be more likely to do the follow up."

"And it worked!" Paul said.

Sharon was quiet, but Annalise felt her appraising stare and looked over. It was obvious that Sharon knew there was more than Annalise was telling everyone. Sharon understood the *I'll tell you later* look in Annalise's eyes and slight nod of her head to not ask in front of the others, and nodded her head in reply.

"Let us know when Susan gets a response," Sarah said.

"I'll save us all some time and send a group text," Annalise said. "Jennifer, these devilled eggs are delicious! What did you put in them?" she went on to make sure the conversation didn't linger on the newspaper story and any questions that might have come up about the logistics of how it would work. *It was just a sin of omission and I'll fill them in about the rest once Paul isn't around,* she told herself when the guilt began to creep in.

"It's a family recipe I am sworn to secrecy not to reveal," Jennifer said, and winked at Annalise.

"Fair enough, but now you realize whenever we want devilled eggs, you will be the one we nominate to make them," which made everyone laugh.

The appetizers were followed by the entrée of fried chicken which Eva made, potato salad which Sharon brought, and a fruit salad from Sarah. The biscuits which Paul brought in a quilted basket had everyone asking if he had made it and where they could find the pattern. Annalise completed the meal with a blueberry pie made with Maine wild blueberries and vanilla ice cream on the side. She hadn't made the ice cream, but no one seemed to mind.

"I'm not sure I'm going to be able to move after all I ate," Eva groaned. "I think we outdid ourselves with this one. It hadn't occurred to me what having two more dishes added to the meal would do for my waistline, but I'm not suggesting we do it differently next week," she said when she realized her remark might have made Paul and Sharon feel unwelcome. "Is anyone up for a walk around the garden to burn off some of these calories before we spend the rest of our time sitting?"

"That sounds like just what we need," Jennifer agreed.

Twenty minutes later, they were back inside in Eva's sewing room, ready to work on their projects.

"Before we begin, I wanted to mention a service at Quilting Essentials I wasn't aware of and maybe none of you were either," Jennifer began. "Paul, jump in anytime if I need correcting. When I took my quilt top to Nicki, she mentioned they rent out the longarm quilting machine they have as a floor model for people who want to do their own quilting and don't own a longarm machine. You have to take a class to learn how to operate it, which costs one hundred dollars for four hours of instruction, but they then give you a credit for four hours' rental, so it ends up being free. The classes only have two people at a time, so it's almost like having a private lesson. I'm thinking of taking the class. There's no way I can afford or have the room for a longarm of my own, but free motion quilting on my home machine isn't the easiest thing to do when it's a larger project. I wanted to pass that along in case anyone else might want to take the class, too. Did I get that all right, Paul?"

"I should add you to the sales staff. That was perfect!"

"I had no idea the longarm was available for customers to rent. I've done a king size quilt on my machine at home, but it was challenging even with the setup I have. Sign me up!" Eva said.

"That would make it so much easier. Even a queen size quilt can be a pain, so I've avoided making any quilts larger than a throw size. I'd be interested in taking the class," Annalise said.

"That would be perfect for me, too. I've wanted to make quilts for my daughters but haven't because the thought of quilting king size quilts to fit their beds on my machine at home made my arms hurt even before I got started. I know I can have it professionally quilted and no offense to Nicki, but I wanted to do it all myself to make it even more of a keepsake," Sharon said.

"Do you offer the classes and rental times on Saturdays? I don't think I would be able to take time off during the week, but I'd love to be able to use the longarm," Sarah asked.

"We don't usually have classes on Saturdays because it can get busy in the store, but we could probably work something out," Paul said. "Would Sunday be an option for you? The store is closed on Sundays, but I'm sure Evelyn would let us use the space with some advance notice."

"Yes, it might be even better for me than a Saturday. Let me know when you've had a chance to talk it over with Evelyn."

"Will do."

"Thank you for telling us about this, Jennifer. It's given me all sorts of ideas for new projects I wouldn't have tackled otherwise," Eva said.

"You're welcome. Maybe we can sign up to take the class together."

"I like that idea. It's a date!"

With that settled, the conversation ended, but the room was soon buzzing with the sounds of sewing machines and the occasional hiss of the steam iron as they each concentrated on their projects.

"Time's up!" Eva announced when her phone alarm went off.

"So soon?" Annalise asked, even though she knew Eva had to be right. "That time flew by, and I didn't think once about treasure maps even though we're working on a treasure box quilt pattern."

"That's one of many things I love about quilting. It takes my mind off all the other things cluttering up my mind," Sarah said.

"I'm the same way. A lot of times I'll put in my AirPods and listen to an audiobook while I'm quilting. That way I can get in some reading time, too," Sharon agreed. "It doesn't work if I'm doing a more difficult quilt block that requires my full attention. I learned that lesson the hard way after having to rip out way too many seams because I stitched them onto the wrong piece."

"Been there, done that," Annalise said.

The evening ended with the drawing of the courses for the next week's potluck and saying their goodbyes. Annalise hung back and caught Sharon's attention to do the same. Once all the others had left, she explained why.

CHAPTER THIRTY-EIGHT

"I didn't want to bring this up while Paul was here, and it would have looked suspicious if I had asked everyone except him to stay. I'll fill in Jennifer and Sarah later so they will be in the loop, too, though. Eva knows some of this, but what I hadn't told you is Jim and I went to the detectives on Timothy Nelson's case to tell them about the plan to arrange to give back the map piece. At first they thought I was only there about the break-in and were ready to tell me to go packing, but I told them the article in the paper is part of a larger plan to catch Timothy's killer. I reassured them Susan doesn't know that part of it either because it would have required more explanation than I wanted to make, so I didn't exactly lie, but I didn't tell her everything. When I showed them the mugshot of Michael and said he was the killer, it got Detective Smith's attention. He had spoken to Michael at the murder scene and recognized him from the photo. He had to look back through his notes, but the name matched. I explained the offer to give the piece of the treasure map back is to lure Michael Granger to meet me in person so I

could tell him I know he's a descendant of Harvey Granger and just like him, he was willing to kill his friend to have the map for himself. Harvey killed John Nelson, and Michael killed John's grandson, Timothy. I would tell him I'd seen him standing over Timothy's body and about the piece of the map sticking out of the wallet beside it. That got their attention, and they wanted to know how I got that information. I had to admit I'd seen it in a vision since it wasn't something I should have known about, but then, of course, that brought up the psychic thing. They weren't happy about it, but I didn't feel I had any other choice to explain how I got that information since there was no reason for me to have been there. They finally accepted I might be on the level and told me they'd do what they can to get approval to go through with my plan."

"You told them you're a psychic?" Sharon asked.

"Yes. I hadn't planned to, but it seemed to be the only way, even though it was risky. Did Jim tell you about that, Eva?" Annalise turned to Eva to ask.

"He did, but I didn't want to say anything until you were ready to talk about it."

"Was he angry? He didn't seem to be, but he didn't say much on the ride home and I was afraid he felt broadsided. I should have talked to him about it then, but it was clear to me he needed to process his feelings first."

Eva chuckled. "He wasn't angry, but you're right about needing to process his feelings. Once he talked it out with me, I think he realized you had to explain how you knew about the wallet and seeing Michael Granger standing over Timothy Nelson's body, which is why you recognized him when you saw his mugshot."

"I'm glad, but I still want to tell him I'm sorry for just blurting it out. It wasn't planned, but still... It took a few days, but I finally got a call yesterday that they got permission to tape Michael when we meet. Susan will set it up, but Detective

Roberts will come with me posing as a friend. Unless he told Jim, he may not know that yet."

"I can tell him," Eva offered.

"Are you sure you should do this? It could be dangerous, even with Detective Roberts with you. This guy has already killed one person over the map," Sharon objected.

"That's why we're going to do it at The Daily Drip coffee shop. We don't think he'd try anything in a public place. As far as he knows, he's just there for me to give him the piece of the map and once he's got it, I'm not a problem anymore. And Detective Roberts will have backup nearby just in case that changes once Michael realizes the real reason he's there."

"Like I said, this could be dangerous," Sharon repeated, and the fear on her face was clear.

"It has to be done," Annalise said quietly, and Sharon knew there was no point trying to talk her out of it.

CHAPTER THIRTY-NINE

~

$\mathcal{T}$he voice in his head just. wouldn't. shut. up.

Why did you give him a piece of the map, Michael? That map is ours.

Why didn't you pick up the piece before you ran?

How could you be so stupid, Michael?

How do you expect to find the treasure if you don't have the rest of the map?

As if that wasn't enough, Bill kept going on and on and on about *poor Tim. Who would want to hurt him? He was a great guy and would have taken the shirt off his back to help someone else... blah blah blah.*

Michael was surprised Bill hadn't started calling him Saint Timothy. He had barely been able to keep it together so he wouldn't blurt out he was the one who had killed Tim just so Bill would shut up. And that Tim had deserved it. *Who did he think he was, making Michael give him a piece of the map?* His *map.*

Michael knew his drinking wasn't helping, but when he was passed out, the voice stopped, and he could have some peace. He didn't have to think about the eviction notice and where he was going to live with no money to pay a deposit on a new apartment. He had looked for work when he was sober enough and the hangover wasn't so bad he could barely move, but no one called back. If he could just find the treasure, all his worries would be over. But he needed the rest of the map. It was one thing to break into that thief, Annalise Jordan's, house again, but getting the piece back that had to be in police custody was going to be impossible. *One problem at a time, Michael. Just get the piece you can, and the rest will fall into place.* How? he kept asking, but the voice was quiet about that. *Figures. When I need you to tell me something, you have nothing to say.*

He looked at the clock and realized he needed to clean up. Bill was coming by in an hour to take him to Tim's memorial service. *Saint Timothy,* he said sarcastically. He had to go even though he was dreading it. They were supposed to have been best friends. It wouldn't look right not to. Not going would raise questions he didn't want to answer. Resigned that he had no other choice, he dragged himself up from the couch and into the bathroom. Maybe a long, hot shower would clear his head. He needed to be on his game if he was going to make it through another afternoon with Bill crying about *poor Tim.*

CHAPTER FORTY

~

Two weeks had passed since the article Susan Reynolds wrote about Annalise wanting to give back her piece of the treasure map was printed in The Bangor News. There hadn't been even a single bite, and logic told her she should probably give up the plan. Everyone, including Detectives Roberts and Smith, told her if Michael Granger was going to take the bait, he would have by now. Still, her intuition disagreed. She had a very strong impression he would make another attempt to get it.

There could be lots of reasons why no one had reached out. Maybe they hadn't even seen the article, she reasoned. She didn't blame the detectives for telling her they had to move on, but to let them know if she did eventually receive a response. They remained positive their investigation would come up with leads to solve the case, but appreciated her offer to help. Annalise could tell even though they hadn't said so, they were relieved her plan hadn't worked. That way, they wouldn't have to reveal a psychic had conned them into participating in a sting that never panned out.

It was time to come up with a Plan B, but no ideas were forthcoming. She had thought for sure the article would draw Michael Granger out, so hadn't anticipated ever needing a Plan B.

A meditation might help and even if she failed to think of an alternate plan, she would feel more relaxed.

It was late afternoon when she went to her sitting room and began her ritual to prepare herself. The day had been warm and sunny, so she opened the window to let in some fresh air before sitting in her chair next to it. The curtains fluttered softly in and out with the breeze, almost as though they were breathing. Sunshine was coming through the window casting diffused beams of light through the sheer fabric of the curtains that warmed and relaxed her body and dust motes were dancing in the air in front of her eyes. Her breath slowed and a sense of calm flowed through her body. She could still smell the incense and heard the music playing, but it was fading to a whisper. Her eyes closed and she leaned her head against the back of the chair.

It was mid-afternoon and she was upstairs when she heard the crunch of gravel as a car pulled into her driveway. Not expecting anyone, she walked to the front window and saw a strange car parked there. She was standing to the side so whoever was in the car wouldn't be able to see her looking down on them. Two men got out and she instantly recognized Michael Granger as the driver. Although she couldn't say with certainty, her instincts told her the other person was Bill Robinson, Frank Abbott's descendant. She watched as they walked to her front door and then the doorbell chimed. Her breathing had quickened when she saw Michael's face, so she took a moment to center herself before going downstairs to open the door. Her intuition told her she should not acknowledge she already knew who they were, even though Michael would know she did after their encounter at the diner. When she was nearly at the bottom of the stairs, the doorbell rang again. *He's nervous and impatient. Be careful,* the voice in her head cautioned.

"May I help you?" she said, smiling as she opened the door.

"Yes, ma'am. We're here about the treasure map," Michael replied, and she saw the challenge in his eyes, daring her to deny knowing why they were there.

"Oh, yes, of course. Please come in," she said, opening the door wider and stepping aside so they could pass by. "Why don't we sit in here where it's more comfortable," she said, leading them into the living room. She gestured for them to take a seat on the couch, and she sat on the chair facing Michael.

"The article in The Bangor News said you have a piece of a treasure map and wanted to give it back to the person who had the other pieces."

"That's right."

"Well, that's me, and that other piece belongs to me. I'd like to have it now," he said, his voice hard and dangerous.

With a start, Annalise's awareness returned to the room, and the vision was gone. It wasn't as threatening as her earlier dream about the visit, but her hands were shaking, and she felt her heart rapidly beating. Taking several deep breaths in and slowly breathing out, her panic subsided. She now knew what she would have to do. And she also realized she could not tell anyone, or they would insist she change her mind.

CHAPTER FORTY-ONE

~

*I*t had been all he could do to sit through Tim's memorial service, but he'd made it. Bill still didn't suspect anything, and the cops hadn't been in touch since the day Tim died, so his performance must have been convincing. He had picked up some day labor jobs and paid his landlord his back rent so he wouldn't be evicted. Or at least not right away. That was the only string of good luck he'd had recently, and his mood was dark. He was flipping through the pages of The Bangor News, skimming the articles but not really registering what he was reading until the headline of one on page four caught his attention.

Do You Have the Missing Pieces of This Treasure Map?

Several weeks ago, we reported the story of a local woman whose great-grandfather had once tried to save the life of a stranger who had appeared on his doorstep in 1926. He had been shot and claimed the person who had done it had also killed their other partner. The killer was still pursuing him because he wanted the remaining piece of a treasure map. Fatally wounded, the man died during the night, and no one ever showed up to claim it. The piece of the treasure map was passed down through the generations and might have forever remained a mystery until the skeletal remains of a body were recently found and an autopsy confirmed gunshot wounds were the likely cause of death. The remains were discovered under a copper-bottomed boat that had resurfaced when the water level of the Kenduskeag River was lowered as a result of the severe drought conditions this year. After reading the story, Annalise Jordan, who is currently in possession of the map, contacted me to tell me the story her family had recounted through the years. The detail about the copper-bottomed boat matched what she had been told. Ms. Jordan has decided she would like to return the piece of the map to the descendants of its original owner. She has contacted me again in the hope that, like herself, that story and the other two pieces of the map have been passed down to the current descendants. If you think you may have them, contact me at The Bangor News to make arrangements for her to return the missing piece. We will require proof the other pieces match the remaining section of the map held by Ms. Jordan.

Maybe my luck has finally turned, Michael thought as his excitement started to build.

It's a trap, sonny boy, he heard in his head, dashing the hope he had begun to feel again. *You know where she lives. You don't have to go through the newspaper. Just show up at her house.*

The logic of that made perfect sense. He would take Bill with him so he would have back up in case The Thief, as he'd begun referring to Annalise in his head, tried anything. He didn't have both pieces to prove they were the missing parts of the map, but if she wouldn't give it to him with just the one piece, he'd take it anyway. And then he'd figure out a way to get back the one Tim had *stolen* from him. In his mind, that was how he saw it. He was going to have to wait a while, though, if it really was a trap. If she thought no one was going to come forward to claim it, she would let her guard down.

CHAPTER FORTY-TWO

～

"Come in," Sharon said, giving Annalise a kiss on the cheek. "Joseph is out on the deck. Why don't we go join him and visit for a bit before we start on the baby quilt project?"

Sharon's daughter, Jessica and her husband, Scott, were having their first baby in September and Annalise had offered to help Sharon pick out a pattern.

"I brought the pattern books I have with baby quilts in them. I know you can find patterns by doing an internet search, but sometimes it's nice to look at them without having to do all the clicking."

"Thanks! We can always use the computer search as Plan B if I don't find something I like."

Joseph stood up to greet them when they walked out onto the back deck.

"Annalise, it's good to see you. I know Sharon has seen you, but I think it's my first time since Mandy's wedding last month."

"Can you believe both your girls are now grown up and

married and Jess will be having her own baby soon?" she asked Sharon.

"It doesn't seem possible, but I couldn't be happier for both of them."

"Are you enjoying your first summer in Maine, Joseph?"

"Arizona will always be my home, but I could get used to summers like this. And everything is so green! We do have places that are green, but it's everywhere here."

"Come back in January. It will be a whole different story."

"I'll take your word for it. I don't think my old bones would tolerate the cold."

"You should come visit us instead. The casita would be like your own private vacation spot, but with the benefit of having us in the main house when you want company or a tour guide," Sharon offered.

"I would love that! I've never visited Arizona, but think I would enjoy it."

"We're going to hold you to that. Just let us know when you're ready. I don't think the kids have any plans to visit this winter between a new baby and just getting married, so it should be available whenever you want to come."

"That sounds wonderful. I'll check with you first when I'm thinking about booking a flight just to make sure, though."

"Perfect! Now that we've got that settled, why don't we go down to my sewing room and try to find a pattern. I might have something in my stash I could use to make it, but who am I kidding? We both know it's more likely I'll be taking a trip to the quilt shop to buy something new."

They both laughed, knowing the truth of that.

Sharon had converted a portion of the finished basement into a sewing room. She had added extra ceiling lighting to offset the lack of windows so it didn't feel cave-like. The walls had been sheet rocked and painted a pale yellow giving it a sunny glow, and the bookcases and sewing cabinet were a bright white. Her fabric organization was very similar to Eva's; all sorted by color and stored in the bookcases. A separate area of the basement was set up as a den and TV space with comfortable seating which they availed themselves of to look through the pattern books Annalise had brought.

"So, what aren't you telling me, Lise?"

"What do you mean?"

"Don't try playing innocent with me. You might be able to fool your quilt club friends, but we're family and we've known each other all our lives. Something is going on with you. I can feel it."

Annalise sighed. She really hadn't wanted to tell anyone about what she'd seen in her meditation, but she knew Sharon wouldn't let it go.

"My spidey senses have been practically screaming at me. I think Michael Granger still wants the map."

"I thought you said no one has been in touch with The Bangor News about it."

"They haven't, but I had a vision he came to my house. And he had someone else with him who I think is Bill Robinson, Frank Abbott's descendant."

"Did you have the feeling you would be in danger?" Sharon asked with concern.

"The vision ended with him saying he wanted the map, but at that point he wasn't threatening me with physical harm."

"That didn't really answer my question," Sharon pushed.

Annalise scowled.

"You know I love you, but you can be really annoying at times," she said.

Sharon just laughed.

"I love you, too. That's why I'm not letting this slide."

"The security company is coming on Tuesday to install the alarm system. He won't be able to break in again without setting it off."

"That makes me feel a little better. You're being extra careful in the meantime?"

"I am. And I'm being honest with you about not thinking I'm in harm's way. Before you say it, I know even someone with psychic abilities doesn't always see bad things coming. I'm convinced he hasn't given up, but if my life was in danger, I think I'd feel differently. It's probably not going to make sense, but I feel confident whatever happens will work out for the best and be in my favor."

"I hope you're right."

"Me, too."

CHAPTER FORTY-THREE

~

*M*ichael hadn't shown Bill the newspaper article when he'd first read it. He didn't want to have to admit he was hearing a voice in his head he believed was Harvey Granger's. Or, that same voice had told him it was a trap and he should wait, but everything was fine now. File that under the Need-to-Know category and Bill didn't need to know. Bill also didn't need to know he hadn't actually called the paper to set up a meeting. The voice was still firm about not giving anyone advance notice he was coming for the map. Now or never, he thought, and called Bill.

"Hey, buddy, how're you doin'?" Bill greeted him.

"I've got some good news. I saw this article in The Bangor News that said Annalise Jordan wants to give her piece of the map to whoever has the other pieces. I called them up, and they set up a meeting with her for this afternoon. I want you to come with me. How about I pick you up around one o'clock?"

"No kidding? I wonder what made her want to do that? It's

too bad Tim isn't here when we finally have the rest of the map," Bill said, his voice turning melancholy.

Michael gritted his teeth so he wouldn't snap at Bill. Thanks to Tim, he now only had one piece of the map and still hadn't figured out how he would get back the one he'd given Tim. *One thing at a time,* he told himself again.

"Yeah, we should have all been in on this. So, can you come?"

"I haven't got anything else going on. Sure, pick me up."

"Great! See you at one."

Michael wanted Bill with him, but now that he'd made up his mind to go, he would have done it by himself if he had to. Still, he breathed a sigh of relief he wouldn't be alone with The Thief. She had seen him at the diner and somehow she recognized him. They hadn't taken anything when they'd broken in, though, and she'd been the one to offer to hand over the piece she had. It should just be a matter of showing up and asking for it. Easy peasy.

CHAPTER FORTY-FOUR

~

The foreshadowing sensation that something was going to happen had come out of nowhere, but Annalise was certain today was the day Michael Granger would make his move. It figured the alarm system wouldn't be installed until tomorrow. She considered leaving for the day, but knew he would break in to steal the map if she was gone. That might get him out of her hair, but she wanted to put an end to this for good, and Timothy Nelson deserved justice for his death. There was no point calling Detectives Roberts and Smith with nothing more substantial than a *tingle* alerting her that Michael was coming. They were already skeptical about the information she'd given them. Whatever happened, and something big was about to happen, she would have to trust she would come out okay on the other side.

CHAPTER FORTY-FIVE

*I*t was two-thirty when she heard the crunch of tires on the gravel in her driveway. Feeling a sense of déjà vu, she walked to the window in the front of her bedroom which faced the driveway, and looked down just as two men were getting out of the car, exactly as it had happened in her vision. She walked back to the end table in her sitting room where she had left her phone. Picking it up, she dialed Detective Smith's number, which she had added to her Favorites list earlier, and was relieved to have him pick up on the first ring.

"Detective Smith, this is Annalise Jordan."

"Have you heard from The Bangor News?"

"No, but Michael Granger and another man, who I believe is Bill Robinson, just pulled into my driveway. Can you send someone to my house right away? It would be best if whoever comes doesn't use their siren or lights to alert them they're coming."

"Are you sure it's him?"

"Yes, I recognized his face from the mugshot photo."

"Do you have a way to leave the house without them seeing you?"

Just as she was about to reply, the doorbell rang.

"I don't think I can. I'm upstairs and I have no way to go to the back of the house from here without passing by the front door which has a sidelight they can see through. It would probably be better if I don't leave. I should go now," she said, and disconnected the call.

Just as had happened in her vision, the doorbell chimed again as she reached the bottom of the stairs. She opened the door to find Michael Granger in front and Bill Robinson behind him and slightly to the right.

"May I help you?"

"Yes, ma'am. We're here about the treasure map," Michael replied, and the feeling of déjà vu washed over her again when she saw the challenge in his eyes, daring her to deny knowing why they were there.

"Oh, yes, of course. Please come in," she said, opening the door wider and stepping aside so they could pass by. "Why don't we sit in here where it's more comfortable," she said, leading them into the living room. She gestured for them to take a seat on the couch. Michael sat at one end of the couch and Bill at the other, and she took a seat on the chair facing Michael. She wanted to make sure the window was behind them so she could see when the police showed up, hopefully without alerting Michael or Bill. *Please let them show up soon* she sent out the silent plea to the Universe.

"The article in The Bangor News said you have a piece of a treasure map and wanted to give it back to the person who had the other pieces."

"That's right."

"Well, that's me, and that other piece belongs to me. I'd like to have it now," he said, his voice hard and dangerous.

She pretended she didn't catch the threatening undertone to

his reply.

"I didn't catch your names."

"My name is Michael Granger, and this is my friend Bill Robinson. We're both descendants of the men who were looking for the treasure."

"Do you have the other pieces with you so I can verify mine is the missing one?"

"I only brought one. I figured that's all you'd need."

"I suppose you're right," she said and smiled. "Wait here and I'll go get it for you."

Trusting they wouldn't follow her, she went to her bedroom and retrieved the map from its secret compartment in the jewelry box. She lingered to try to buy time for the police to arrive, but not long enough to raise Michael's suspicions. She could tell from Bill Robinson's demeanor he was not part of Michael's deception, but she would still need to be careful.

"May I see your piece?" she asked when she returned.

Michael pulled it from his wallet and unfolded it on the coffee table between them. She unfolded her piece and aligned it to the spot where it had been removed.

"It fits," Michael said with decisiveness. "I'll just take that back and your piece, too," he said, holding out his hand.

Annalise handed them over.

"When did you plan to tell Bill that you don't really have the other piece? You gave it to Timothy just before you killed him."

Michael's face lost all its color, and their eyes locked.

"What's she talking about, Mike?" Bill asked.

"The old bat is crazy. I left the other piece in my apartment," Michael said. "Come on, let's go."

He started to rise, but hesitated when a disembodied voice coming from behind Annalise told him to sit back down. This time, both Michael's and Bill's faces blanched when they saw the figure of a man standing there, his body translucent at first, but then became opaque.

CHAPTER FORTY-SIX

~

*M*ichael fell back on the couch, his eyes wide and his mouth dropped open in surprise.

"Are you seeing what I'm seeing?" Bill asked Michael, his voice barely a whisper.

"Where'd that guy come from?" Michael asked, his voice shaky.

"My name is Frank Abbott. You have Marian's eyes," he said to Bill. "And you have Harvey's bad temper," he directed at Michael. "He wasn't always that way, but after he got it in his head to find the treasure, it was like he became possessed. The gold fever got him. I don't think he would have killed John and me if it wasn't for that. And now you've got it," he said to Michael. "You killed your friend, Timothy, after he made you give him the piece of the map. The one you claim you have in your apartment."

Annalise remained quiet, barely daring to breathe as she let the scene play out. She looked behind her and unlike when Sarah had been in contact with Frank, she could now see and hear him.

Inwardly, she was praying the police would arrive before Michael used violence to escape from the corner he'd been put in by her and Frank.

"Are they telling the truth, Mike? Did you kill Tim?" Bill's voice was quiet but hard as he looked at his friend who was still shaken by what the man had said.

"I had to do it. The map is *mine*, and he was trying to steal it from me," he answered, his voice defiant. "I didn't intend to shoot him. It just happened." He looked pleadingly at Bill, but when he did not get any sympathy from him, his voice turned cold. "I'll shoot both of you, too, if I have to," and reached into the waistband of his jeans and pulled out the gun he'd used to kill Tim, brandishing it first in Bill's direction and then at Annalise. "Sit over there in the other chair," he snarled at Bill, who moved over to the chair next to Annalise.

"You need to forget about the map and the treasure. They're cursed. Don't give in to the fever. You can still redeem yourself," Frank tried reasoning with him.

"It's too late! Can't you see that? I killed Tim and I have to kill them, too, or I won't get away with it so I can find the gold!" he shouted at Frank. More subdued and sounding petulant, he continued. "It's all her fault. Bill would never have known about Tim if she hadn't opened her big mouth. We could have found the treasure, and everything would have been fine."

"Open up!! It's the police," they heard at the door and Michael's head whipped around in that direction.

CHAPTER FORTY-SEVEN

~

"Come on," Annalise whispered to Bill as she bolted out of her chair and ran toward the kitchen to escape out the back door. Frank was no longer standing there, but she heard the sound of a scuffle behind them as they ran.

"Drop the gun!" she heard someone shout from the front of the house as she flung open the door and ran out, with Bill right behind her.

The next few minutes were a blur for her as several police cars careened into her driveway, blocking Michael's car from leaving. Two policemen ran around to the back of the house and went in the door she and Bill had just used to escape while two others had entered through the front door, which she had left unlocked to make it easier for them to come in. At last, Michael was being led out of the house in handcuffs with a policeman on either side of him, and Annalise finally relaxed. It was then that an unmarked car pulled in with Detectives Roberts and Smith. They walked over to Annalise after they'd identified themselves to one of the other cops.

"Are you alright?" Smith asked her.

"A little shaken, but I'm okay."

"Who are you?" Roberts asked Bill.

"Bill Robinson. Michael brought me here, but I had no idea he had a gun. I thought we were just here to get the map. He told me The Bangor News had set it up."

"He's telling the truth," Annalise said.

"Were you with him during the first break-in at Ms. Jordan's house?"

"Yes," he answered, looking embarrassed. "But we didn't take anything," he added quickly.

Detective Smith started to Mirandize Bill, but Annalise interrupted.

"Is there any way you can let that go? Nothing was stolen and other than having things dumped on the floor, there wasn't any damage to the house."

Detective Smith thought for a moment. "I guess in that case, it could be considered trespassing and if you don't want to press charges, we can overlook it. You don't have any intention of returning, do you?" he asked, turning to Bill.

"No, sir. I don't want anything to do with that map or the treasure ever again!"

"That's good enough for me. As for what happened today with Michael Granger, though, I think you're going to want to hear this," she said, pulling her phone out of the pocket of her skirt and holding it up for them to see.

"What's that for?" Roberts asked.

"I'm getting pretty good at using voice memos," she said with a smile.

"Why don't you take Mr. Robinson over to the car to get his statement, Dennis," Roberts said, "and I'll find out what else Ms. Jordan has to tell us about what happened here."

As soon as they were out of earshot, he pointed to the phone

Annalise still held in her hand. "Why don't you play the voice memo for me?"

She unlocked the phone and navigated to the voice memo app. After it finished playing, Roberts had a puzzled look on his face.

"Whose voice is that other guy? I thought it was just the three of you inside."

"He was behind me, so I don't know where he had come from, and he wasn't there when Bill and I made our escape, even though we went in that direction. He said he was Frank Abbott."

"Isn't that the name of the guy who showed up here back in 1926?"

"That's the one," Annalise answered, looking him directly in the eyes.

Roberts's head dropped, and he shook it from side to side. Annalise could tell that in his head he was asking the question, *How am I supposed to explain that?* but he remained quiet. He only sighed and then looked back at Annalise with a resigned expression on his face.

"How about you tell me what happened after you called Detective Smith?"

"Of course. Do you think we can go inside now?"

"Wait here. I'll check with one of the officers." He walked away and as he passed by Detective Smith, he gave another of those shakes of his head as though to say *you're not going to believe this.*

Two hours later, the police had taken Michael Granger away and released Bill Robinson. Once Michael had been taken into custody, it was as though the spell was broken. He confessed to Tim's murder and vouched for Bill's claim that he had known nothing about the murder or Michael's intent for coming today. Michael's car was impounded, and a tow truck arrived to take it away, which left Bill with no way to return home until one of the officers agreed to give him a ride. Once they left, Annalise was alone with the detectives.

Roberts handed her phone back to her. "I don't think we'll be needing this since Granger confessed, but you should probably save the recording until we get back to you."

"That's no problem. I'd be happy to do that."

Dennis Smith gave her a look and then said, "I'll be honest, I hope we don't have to hear it again."

Annalise smiled. "I can understand why you wouldn't."

They both nodded their goodbyes and returned to their car, leaving her alone.

CHAPTER FORTY-EIGHT

~

he next meeting of The Cozy Quilts Club was held two days after Annalise's ordeal. She was the last to arrive and was greeted with hugs and concern for her well-being. She had already received calls from each of them to make sure she was okay, but it felt good to have the physical connection.

"Paul called earlier to let me know he couldn't make it tonight. He and Nicki had already made other plans," Eva told them when they were all gathered at her dining room table. "How are you holding up, Annalise?"

"I'm fine, really," she reassured them. "Honestly, I'm glad it happened because I can feel safe at last now that Michael Granger is behind bars."

"Tell us what happened from the beginning," Eva said.

Annalise proceeded to tell them all the details of what had happened that day. When she finished, the expressions on the faces of the other women all registered a combination of concern and shock as they processed their feelings and the realization of just how precarious her situation had been settled in.

"When I heard the news report, I knew you'd been in a tough spot, but I had no idea just how dangerous it was for you." Jennifer was the first one to break the silence.

"I can't believe you let them in without having anyone else with you," Sharon proclaimed before Annalise had a chance to respond to Jennifer.

Annalise knew Sharon's tone might have been interpreted as a rebuke by anyone else, but she recognized it as the concern of someone who had been frightened for the safety of one they loved.

"I didn't feel like I had a choice. If I hadn't answered the door, they might have broken in. Given the circumstances, letting them in but calling Detective Smith first seemed like the better option," she said, smiling to let Sharon know she understood her concern.

"Alright, I can see your logic and I admit it turned out for the best but I don't have to like how it happened."

"And that's okay, too," Annalise said and walked over to Sharon to give her a hug.

Thinking back about that day after she'd returned to her seat, Annalise continued with another recollection.

"When the officers brought Michael out in handcuffs, it was like he was a completely different person. Have you watched movies and TV shows where someone has been possessed by some entity and when that's gone, they've changed?" Annalise asked.

Everyone nodded.

" I swear it was exactly like that."

There was more silence as everyone thought about what Annalise had told them.

"The rest of our meeting is going to be anti-climactic after hearing all of that, but we should probably wrap up the night with our show and tell of our projects," Eva said, breaking the silence and everyone brought theirs out to share. There were oohs and ahhs for each, and the evening came to its conclusion.

"Well, I don't know how things could be any more exciting than they have the last two months, but I'm looking forward to starting a new project next week," Eva said.

As the others echoed their enthusiasm, Annalise felt the familiar prickle of her skin alerting her there would be more to come and smiled to herself but said nothing.

EPILOGUE

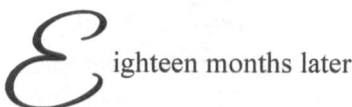ighteen months later

ANNALISE WAS FINISHING her morning coffee when she received a call from Susan Reynolds.

"Susan, what a nice surprise!"

"Hi, Annalise! I would have called you about this earlier, but by the time I was finished getting all the facts and turned in my story, it was too late in the day to call you. Have you read The Bangor News yet?"

"I was just about to check it out. What should I be looking for?"

"It's on the front page. The treasure was found!"

"What? When?" Annalise asked, stunned by the news.

"A few days ago, but I didn't get a call from the person who found it until last night. He's a history professor and amateur treasure hunter. Our own local Indiana Jones, if you can believe it. He decided to contact me to break the story because it was my articles about the treasure map that led him to discovering its whereabouts. Apparently, he had a journal that was reputed to be written by Dixie Bull and it had another drawing of the treasure map."

"You're kidding! Where did he get it?"

"He's been researching Dixie Bull for years and came across the journal in an antique store down on the Coast. He wasn't sure if it was genuine, but he was able to authenticate the age of the journal to that time period. He hadn't thought about looking for the treasure until after reading the story and subsequent reports about Michael Granger's trial. He said he never expected to find it but had to try just in case. You're never going to believe where he found it."

"Was it really here in Glen Lake?" Annalise asked.

"It was! And not just in Glen Lake, it was only a half mile from your house. It was in a section of land that still hasn't been developed and the landowner gave him permission to look for it. The chest was small and made of metal, so he was able to detect it using a special metal detector that can find metals buried at deeper distances than your run-of-the-mill ones."

"I have to ask, how close was it to where the boat was found?"

"If they had walked about three hundred feet from where they came ashore, they probably would have found it. The chest was filled with gold coins that are worth a small fortune," Susan said.

"What is the treasure hunter going to do with it?" Annalise asked. The thought occurred to her that it might not have been just the map that was cursed; the gold might have been, too.

"I'll be honest with you; I was shocked to learn he intends to donate it to the Maine State Museum to set up an exhibit about Dixie Bull. He wasn't just a treasure hunter, though. I don't know if being a history professor and wanting to contribute to the preservation of Dixie Bull's legacy was the only reason he gave it away. He didn't come right out and say so, but I got the impression that he might have believed it would be bad luck to hang onto the gold, considering how many lives were lost because of it. He plans to write a book, though."

"I wish him luck."

They said their goodbyes and Annalise realized she was at last feeling closure. The treasure had been real, but best of all, the spell of the map's allure was broken and no more lives would be lost finding the treasure.

Excerpt from Summer's End
A Cozy Quilts Club Mystery
Book 3

Prologue

"I really should have done this earlier," Summer Williams said out loud although no one else was with her. She was only a mile from her house, but already sweating, and her tee shirt was starting to cling to her back. She looked up at the brilliant azure blue sky hoping to see clouds but there was not a one in sight to deflect the intensity of the sun. The day started out comfortably, but the temperature and humidity on this late August mid-afternoon had climbed by the time she decided to take a run. The baseball cap she had put on to stop the sun from beating on her head helped to shade her eyes and face but even it wasn't enough. She wiped away a bead of sweat trickling its way downward from her forehead toward her temple to keep it from running into her eyes.

Summer was heading into her senior year of high school and had been on the school's track team for the past three years. It was not a guarantee she would be selected for a varsity spot again, though, so taking a day off from her training wasn't negotiable. Making the varsity team was goal number one, but what she really wanted to accomplish was running in the Boston Marathon the following April. It would be her first time and she needed to be prepared physically and mentally.

The only sounds were the pounding of her footsteps on the pavement of the rural road, the occasional squawks of crows overhead, and crickets in the grass beside the shoulder. Her blonde ponytail that she had threaded through the gap in the back of her baseball cap swung back and forth with the rhythm of her steps. She had thought about wearing her AirPods to listen to music while she ran to keep her distracted from the fatigue which hit about an hour into the run, but her mother had been on her case again. It was her preference that Summer use the tread-mill in their basement, but compromised by insisting she not wear the AirPods so she would be focused on any approaching cars. Though the houses on this part of Glen Lake were more spaced-out than other areas, the road which cut through here was a secondary route to several nearby towns, which meant it still had a lot of traffic. In some sections sharp curves prevented a driver from seeing what might be around the corners and they were more likely to be looking for oncoming cars than pedestri-ans. As Summer neared one of those, she thought she could hear a car, but it sounded like it was still in the distance. She calcu-lated how long it would take, and decided she would have no trouble making it to the curve and getting past it before the vehicle reached her. As she rounded the curve, she tried to make sense of what she was seeing. The car had gotten closer faster than she'd anticipated which surprised her, but the bigger shock was that it had no driver. Her brain was still processing this as she moved over to the shoulder of the road, wary now and unsure of what to do, but thinking she might have to jump into the grassy area beyond the shoulder even though it sloped down into a gully. Although it had been going straight, as the car was nearly upon her it was drifting off the pavement and onto the shoulder. She'd waited too long. The car's front fender clipped her right side, and she was thrown into the air, landing in the gully and hidden by the overgrown grass.

Lunch at Nancy's had been exactly what she needed to get

out of her end of summer slump. She hadn't laughed that much in months. The food was mouth-watering delicious and the wine! Had she had two glasses or three? None is what she should have had, but the DUI on her record happened five years ago. Surely it wasn't something to worry about now. She was driving just fine and only felt a little buzzed. No need to be concerned.

She was going a little faster than the speed limit, but the traffic was light today. She hadn't seen another vehicle on the road for miles. The radio's volume was loud, and she was bouncing with the beat, doing her best car dance to match her mood. It was a hot day, and the air conditioning was on full blast; another reason for having the music turned up. She'd forgotten to plug in her phone to enable the hands-free feature and it was still in her purse on the passenger seat. The ringing startled her and even though she knew she shouldn't, she glanced away from the road to try to pull it out to see who was calling and it slipped onto the floorboard. She looked back up to the road and when she appeared to still be going straight and no cars were coming, she bent over to pick up her purse to put it back on the seat. She would have to be quick about it as she was getting close to the curve up ahead; so she slowed down her speed to give herself more time. When she felt the impact and a loud thud sounded from the passenger side, she reflexively yanked the steering wheel to the left and popped back up to find she had drifted toward the shoulder. Once fully back on the pavement she jammed on the brakes, her tires screeching. Her eyes flew to the rearview mirror, but nothing was on the road. Confused, she was certain she hadn't imagined it but if she did hit something, where was it? *It must have been an animal that came out of the bushes and then ran back. If I killed it, it would be lying on the road,* she rationalized. She'd heard accounts of that happening many times over the years, especially when it involved a deer. *Even if I went back, what could I do about it if it was still there?* The argument worked and though her cheerful mood was now history, and her conscience wasn't completely buying it, she continued on her way home, paying closer attention to the road. Her purse would have to stay where it was until then and if whoever had been calling tried again, they would just have to leave a voice mail.

ALSO BY MARSHA DEFILIPPO

Arizona Dreams

Deja vu Dreams

Disillusioned Dreams

A Cozy Quilts Club Mystery series

Follow the Crumbs

Coming January 2024

Summer's End

ABOUT THE AUTHOR

After retiring from her day job of nearly 33 years, Marsha DeFilippo has embarked on a new career of writing books. She is also a quilter and lifelong avid crafter who has yet to try a craft she doesn't like. She spends her winters in Arizona and the remainder of the year in Maine.

For more information, please visit my website:
marsha defilippo.com

To get the latest information on new releases, excerpts and more, be sure to sign up for Marsha's newsletter.
https://marshadefilippo.com/newsletter

facebook.com/Marsha-DeFilippo

twitter.com/marshadefilippo

instagram.com/marshadefilippo

amazon.com/author/marshadefilippo

bookbub.com/authors/marsha-defilippo

pinterest.com/defilippo0699

www.ingramcontent.com/pod-product-compliance
Lightning Source LLC
Chambersburg PA
CBHW030335180626
46810CB00003B/1367